AF440131

The Christmas Committee

LILY SEABROOKE

*For everyone out there
who's been told to give up
but is a bit confused
what that even means
or why you'd do
something silly like that*

Chapter 1

PIPER

Oh, God, I was late. As if things weren't ruined enough. I took the stairs down two at a time, the ice-cold air biting my lungs as I rushed, nearly slipping on one of the steps, iced over in places. It wouldn't have been left to ice over in the old days—this square, this whole place, had fallen apart in the past five years.

I stopped outside the hotel, collecting myself, drawing a deep breath and pulling my coat tighter. *Powerful people show up a few minutes late all the time.* Just brush it off like powerful people did, I told myself. I pictured myself as a formidable executive, coming in a few minutes late because I'd been resolving some other crisis, and everyone would know right away the only reason I was late was because I was *so* important.

Somehow, I wasn't totally sure this was going to fly. But I had to try something. Let it never be said Piper Fairway was the kind of girl to give up.

I pushed open the door and strode with my best important-person walk through the lobby and past the desk, where Rose was on reception, an older woman with long, gray hair she took meticulous care of. She smiled at me.

"How are you doing, Piper?" she said. "Mister Landgrave is waiting for you in the meeting room. Good luck. We're all rooting for you."

"Thanks, Rose." I paused. "Do you ever get impostor syndrome when you're in an important role? You know, just... asking. Hypothetically."

She smiled sweeter. "You'll do fine, honey. There's no one better suited for this than you."

Well, hello again, impostor syndrome. I forced a smile that probably looked about as real as a reality TV model's spray tan, and I headed in through the creaky old door into the meeting room.

"Good afternoon, Mister Landgrave, thanks for waiting," I said as soon as I came in, and he instantly shut down any perceptions of power I might have had—he sat on the other side of a plasticky old table, leaning way back in his chair, on his phone, and he shushed me with a gesture like I was some annoying intern here to deliver a report.

"Really," he said, looking out the window and nodding along with the voice over the phone. "Well, you can bring in Outrider Co. They should be able to get the renovations done."

Meekly, I sat down across from him and folded my hands in my lap.

"Right. Look, Dave, I trust you can handle negotiations. I don't pay you for nothing, do I?" He rolled his eyes. "All right. Yeah. Let me know. Bye."

"Thanks for your patience, Mister Landgrave, I—" I started, but he turned to me, setting the phone down, and spoke over me as if I hadn't said a word.

"Hi, Piper. We've worked it out and three point two is the price. You can sign all the papers here to get it cleared."

I fumed internally. I was not going to look important today.

Michael Landgrave was a man in his late fifties with delicate round glasses and thin, graying stubble, his forehead looking like terraced rice paddies. He wore a pinstriped dress shirt tucked into khaki pants, a brown belt, all casual, which somehow made it more insulting, like the negotiation to buy the heart of our town and tear it down was just a casual lunch trip for him.

I sat up straighter, trying to picture myself as the fiery protagonist in a movie who refused to let her town die. "I'm not signing papers," I said. "Mister Landgrave, I, um—I don't intend to sell today." I faltered. "Or tomorrow, either, for that matter."

He raised his eyebrows, incredulity all over him. "You want a higher price than three point two? Even that's generous, you know. Land valuations have cut almost in half over the past ten years here."

I swallowed hard, but I shook my head. "No, I don't... it's not about the price. I'm here to tell you that we're, um... not selling. No matter what."

These things kept sounding *so much* more confident in my head. Saying them out loud, I sounded like a five-year-old arguing for why she deserved more cookies.

Mister Landgrave waved me off. "I understand the situation, right. I know how things work. Nothing is ever for sale until you offer enough. So, let's go through the specific valuations of everything I'm placing an offer on, and we'll see why three point two is actually quite generous."

"This isn't about *valuations*—"

"To start, I'm buying the center complex, which is of course the main part of this," he said. "Now, I see why you'd think it's worth a lot. It's a big building, old architecture, some fine work. But that's also our drawback. That kind of old architecture is quite expensive to restore. It's a sunk cost more than anything else. I honestly would have guessed a million, one point five when I saw it, but my expert appraisers pointed out some money sinks. We're looking at six hundred for that one."

"Um… Mister Landgrave, I don't think you're listening to me."

He leaned over the table and set down a map, unrolling it to show an aerial view of Castle Hollow, red markings clustered around the town center. "This strip here is actually our largest expenditure," he said. "These buildings are all a bit newer and in better condition, which is a bonus for us."

"How is it a bonus if you're just tearing them all down anyway?"

"Newer construction comes down more cleanly."

I scowled at him. "Look, I need you to listen. We're not selling any of this."

He sank back in his squeaky little office chair that might have been from the nineties with a sigh. "Piper. Look, I get it. This is your town. It's important to you. But I don't want you to think of this as an ending. This is a new beginning. Castle Hollow is going to see an incredible revitalization. It's going to become a luxurious suburb, and once that happens, I can promise you a *lot* of money is going to come flowing in. Local businesses are going to come to life. Your home values are going to go up. And this investment project is going to put you—all of you—on the map."

"We don't *want* to be on the map. We're doing perfectly well as we are."

He scoffed. "I have access to a computer and a brain, Piper. I can read statistics. Where should we start? Average income has fallen thirty percent in the past five years. Home values have dropped through the floor, but there's still a net outflow of people moving away. And the cultural board? How many members are on it now?"

I cleared my throat. "Um... Whitney is technically—"

"Right, so it's just you."

I hung my head.

"It's a shame, Piper. Really, it is. All across America, small towns like this are dying. I empathize—I do. I visited Castle Hollow for Christmas once, seven years back. The place was magical."

"Right?" I lit up just a little, thinking of the old Christmas celebrations. The whole plaza lit up, a Christmas market aglow with aromas of spice and candied orange, music and laughter filling the air. Shops inside the plaza all alive with activity, the ice-skating rink packed full, children lined up to sit on Santa's lap under the big Christmas tree in the center complex.

"Christmas magic, embodied," he said. "Like walking through the pages of a storybook. But those days are long gone, aren't they?"

I winced. "Yes… well. That's been my work on the cultural board, to try bringing that magic back."

"The form magic takes changes over the years," he said. "No sense trying to chase the image of what it looked like once upon a time. Let's embrace the now. Castle Hollow has fallen apart trying to be what it can't be anymore. Before the rest of the town falls through, before everyone else leaves and it's just you trying to hold the curtains up, let's give it some magic back."

I scowled. I had officially just hit the point of *fed up* with this man. "You talk a lot about magic, for someone who looks like a dollar-store version of the most boring businessman alive."

He blinked. I kept going.

"I'm not signing off on anything that involves you—tearing down our culture and our history and the heart of our community and building a road big enough to live in, a bunch of cookie-cutter McMansions and—" I stood up. "I don't care what you're saying or what you're offering. Please don't come back. Castle Hollow is just fine without you."

He raised his eyebrows high. "Do you know the tourism board is coming through?"

I stopped, suddenly losing my momentum. "Um... what?"

"Yes. They've still been recommending Christmas at Castle Hollow, to come experience the magic. But they've heard plenty about how it's been falling apart here, so... this year, they're coming through to see for themselves. And I think the cultural grant will depend on what they see."

"I—um." I scratched my head, suddenly in a nervous panic. Despite everything I said, I knew full well the tourism board would cook us alive if they saw the state of things lately.

"I hope you're not relying on that cultural grant too much."

"No, um..." I fussed with my collar. We were relying on that cultural grant a lot. And I think Mister Landgrave knew that.

"I understand you want to carry on as you have been. But that's not really one of the options," he said, leaning back in his seat with that insufferable *I've-won* smile on his face. "You're already in very deep trouble. What I'm offering you is a way out. Let us buy up the property, and we'll make Castle Hollow into a place people will be happy to call home, again and again."

I took a long breath. Gloria had told me to do my best with the negotiations, but she'd had a resolved look like she figured selling was inevitable. People had been talking a lot about the city center and its old Christmas celebrations like they were a bygone, never to return. It was probably inevitable that I caved and signed the papers.

So I gathered all my wits, pulled myself together as best I could, and I said, "Go shove a cactus up your ass."

He blinked, twice, slowly. "I beg your pardon?"

But I turned and walked out the door instead, huffing the whole way, and shut the door hard behind me.

Chapter 2

LYRA

Castle Hollow had been sold as charming and sweet, full of character. I felt like I ordered small-town charm off Wish.

I drove slow past the city center, looking over the ghost town, and I just got sadder the more I saw—old buildings all run-down with shuttered storefronts, a too-small Christmas tree in the center of the plaza that might have had two or three whole lights on it. It looked like there'd been a terrible incident, and everyone had been forced to flee town while in the middle of setting up the Christmas decorations.

Didn't matter. Not terribly much, anyway. I was only landing here for a month. At least until things blew over with Sonia, and I could go back. I'd been hoping to at least spend Christmas in a place with some damn Christmas cheer, but it had always been a rotten, lousy holiday for me anyway. What did it matter at this point?

When I arrived at the house I'd rented, it didn't inspire much more confidence, either. A rundown place on the hill—I had to admit the view was beautiful, but only as long as your back was turned to the house. I parked in the driveway under the creaking eaves of the house, and I pulled my scarf tighter before I stepped out of the car, breathing in the fresh, crisp wintry air.

The sound, the scenery—it felt like there was nobody around for miles, like the world was laid out just for me. I wondered if it was glorious or depressing.

The hill at the front sprawled out over the view of the frozen lake, surrounded by pine trees where it soared up into sharp cliffs on the opposite side. Wind murmured over the frosty expanse and rustled the snow-capped boughs of pine trees around me, and after standing there for a good, long while looking out at it all, I decided that yeah, solace would be good for me right now.

I wanted to be away from everything, if only for right now. I knew before long I'd want to be back with people, but while everything with Sonia was still going on back home? While half the city still thought I was a lying, cheating bitch? I just wanted to be alone, left to do my work in peace.

And so I was immeasurably disappointed to find someone in my house.

I turned back and went up the creaky old steps on the porch that felt like it would fall out underneath me, and I found my first problem when it turned out the door was unlocked. I had to shove it to get it unstuck from the frame, and when I stepped into drafty air and dusty shafts of light through the windows, I heard someone—a woman's voice, muttering frantically to herself from the kitchen. I paused in the foyer, my mind racing wildly.

Did I show up in the middle of a break-in? Was it the owner here trying to fix up this sorry shack before their first tenant in sixty years arrived? Did I show up at the wrong house?

Wisdom would have dictated I turn around and leave, maybe hide out in the car with the lights off and creep to see if anyone came out of the house. But maybe I just didn't have a lot of survival instinct left in me after the nightmare that was my breakup, and I crept carefully through the hallway and into the living room, where I spotted a petite, redheaded woman in the kitchen fumbling with what looked like... it looked like she was trying to fix the sink. She didn't seem to notice me. I contented myself to lean against the peeling, musty wallpaper and watch her.

She looked a little young to be the owner. She might have been... twenty-five. I would have expected a couple of empty-nesters in their seventies. She was pretty, at least. If I had a cute redhead coming over as part of the rental, it would soften the blow just a little.

"I swear, the more I tighten it, the worse it gets," she muttered, twisting at a bolt. "What am I supposed to *do* with this thing?"

"You could try loosening it," I said, and she screamed, dropped the wrench, and evidently broke something, judging by the way the sink sprayed water at her face. She fumbled trying to turn it off, stumbled back away from the sink and tripped over her toolbox, and somehow all in a whirl of clatter and commotion, she collapsed against a windowpane that popped from its frame and fell out, landing in the snow and letting in a sudden burst of freezing air.

This house was worse than I thought. And I'd thought it was bad.

The water petered out, and I crouched by the woman, who was alternately nursing the spot on the back of her head where she'd hit the window and trying to squeeze the water from her hair. "Are you okay?" I said, and she coughed, wiping water from her face.

"I have never been better. This is the best day of my life." She shivered. "So! I guess you're Beth's tenant, huh? Um... welcome to Castle Hollow!"

I blinked. "So... you're the welcoming committee, here to take my sink apart."

She dusted herself off and stood up on shaky footing. "Beth is, um... not the best landlord. She told me she had a tenant coming in for December and asked if I could fix the place up a little for her before you arrived, since she couldn't get up the hill anymore. So... here I am. Hi. I'm Piper."

I looked her over skeptically. If she was a mechanic, she didn't look the part. She was pretty, with long red hair she had in a half-updo, now dripping in the front half, natural makeup that was now a little smudged and dripping, but still pretty. Deep brown eyes with long lashes, a little pout to her lips. She looked more designer than mechanic, especially wearing a slim, chic turtleneck and plaid jacket—all sprayed with water now, of course.

She shivered in the cold air coming in through the window, probably freezing with her dripping hair. I could save idle chat for another time, when we weren't freezing in here. "If you're a handywoman, then I'm sure you'll be happy to help get this window back in the frame before we both freeze to death."

She laughed nervously. "I'm pretty much the exact opposite of a handywoman. I'm a professional at getting in the way and making a mess of things, but I do my best, and I've been called most likely to succeed. I didn't ask who the other candidates were, though. I don't think it'd be a flattering comparison."

"Okay, Piper. Why don't we just focus on the broken window? You look like you're about to go blue."

She made a face at the window. "It looks like it's been popped in and out a million times... I swear I've *told* Beth about this kind of thing."

Just like she said, it did just pop back in. And just like she said, Piper was useless, standing on the side with her hands in her pockets just watching. When I finished wrestling the window back into the frame—it sat crooked and ill-fitting, cold air slipping in around the corners—Piper puffed out her chest and put on a smile.

"So," she said, "that's taken care of."

"She says, with the confidence of someone who had absolutely no part in taking care of it."

She laughed it off. "No arguments there. Beth said your name was Lyla, right?"

"Lyra."

"You'd be the third person to have Beth get your name wrong." She beamed, and honestly— she wasn't scoring a lot of points in the positives column so far, but she had probably the world's most disarming smile, eyes glowing, a little crease at the corners. I relaxed a little without even meaning to. "Thanks for coming to Castle Hollow, Lyra. I'm the head of the cultural committee with the Castle Hollow Directory Commission."

"*Commission* is a very powerful word."

"Gloria's the one who picked all the new names. She's got a penchant for the dramatic."

I leaned back against the counter, but when it creaked, I stood up straight again. "So, the head of the cultural committee spends her time… fixing people's houses."

She cleared her throat, looking away. "Um… when I said I'm the head of the cultural committee, I'm actually also the only one on the committee."

"Ah. Head by default."

"Remember what I said about the other candidates for *most likely to succeed?* Winning by default is my modus operandi." She shook her head. "We used to have a lot more people, but, um… well, Castle Hollow's kind of been in decline recently, you know. So it's been dwindling. In case you were wondering, yes, it's very depressing to hold an election for board head when you're the only person in the room. I stood up at the front of the room, gave a speech, and then went to the other side of the room and made a note that the speech was heard, cast my vote... went over to a third side of the room, tallied the votes... turned out I'd won one hundred percent of the vote."

"Why not—you know—just dissolve the committee and fold its duties into something else?"

Her face reddened. "I can't do that, Lyra. It would be sacrificing the culture and the very soul of Castle Hollow."

"I'm going to be honest with you, Piper, I drove through the town center on my way here—I don't think there's much left to sacrifice."

That one, too, she took in stride, laughing nervously. "Um... touché. But like... you've got to try, right? When everything else is falling through, you've got to at least give it one more shot."

I looked out the window, gazing out over the sweeping expanse past the hill. The cold white skies of a winter afternoon, the endless quiet...

Maybe I was here because I *didn't* want to give things *at least one more shot.* I hadn't really put up much of a fuss with Sonia, if I was being honest with myself.

It was easier to just let go and roll with the punches. Trying to change the world and everyone around us was a fool's errand compared to just moving to where the waters were smoother.

But that wasn't the most important part. "I still don't see what this has to do with being in my house."

She cleared her throat. "The job of the cultural committee is to make Castle Hollow more attractive and appealing for people to visit, live in, and invest in. So... Beth said since you're moving in, I should take it upon myself to help make it a more appealing place, so you'd be more inclined to stay."

I put my hands in my pockets. "I'm only here for the month."

Her face fell. "Only what?"

"And Beth knew that full well when I rented the place. She was just using you to get some repairs on her house."

She looked down. "Oh... that makes sense."

Poor girl. Suddenly she was less annoying and more pitiable. Seemed like she was a people-pleaser and got sucked into being the doormat for everyone in this town—all just baiting her along telling her she'd better do what they want if she wants to save the town.

I was probably going to be bored to death in this place, anyway. I'd expected a *little* bit of a community here, even if it was just old ladies who talked about what their grandchildren were doing these days or gossiping about neighbors. It looked like I was completely out of luck, and I knew if I had nothing to do, I'd spend all my time hunched over a laptop doing extra work I wouldn't even be paid for, so I was honestly happy for something to do.

"You're a bit of a pushover, huh?" I said, and she scrunched up her face.

"You don't need to make it sound like I'm some kind of loser. I just take my work very seriously."

"You take the jobs everyone else wanted to pawn off onto somebody else very seriously. Give yourself a break."

She looked away. "I'm busy."

"Then take a break with me. Let's grab coffee and you can step away from all the chaos and say it's to give a new resident a warm welcome."

Piper went wide-eyed, staring at me for a few seconds, before she said, "Lyra, are you taking pity on me?"

"Yeah. You look like a kicked puppy."

Her jaw dropped. "I—didn't expect such a straightforward response."

"So, how about it?"

She stared at me for a few seconds before she looked down. "Um... that'd be nice, actually. I don't get a lot of opportunities to talk about my work. Do you mind hearing me talk? Like, a lot?"

I gestured around me. "I'm already deathly bored out here, so please do."

She straightened her back, putting a hand to her chest, and I swear the woman positively glowed. "In that case, you can leave it to me! No resident will go dissatisfied or lonely as long as I, Piper Fairway, still draw breath. Tomorrow at ten o'clock, Baron's Coffee, and I will buy you three different types of croissant, and you will love all three of them."

"I work in the mornings. Until noon."

She faltered. "Um... do you want to just trade numbers and you can text me when you're ready?"

I felt a smile coming on. I needed to get away from everything, but I was still the kind of person who needed something to do. Trying to get Piper's head out of the sky wouldn't be the worst use of my time. Especially not if I got to sit across from her and... well, admire the view a little.

I'd been with Sonia two and a half years, and truthfully speaking, I'd gotten bored. If we were going to have a bad breakup, I could at least admire the scenery. And Piper was some nice scenery. I'd always had a weakness for redheads.

"Sounds good," I said.

Chapter 3
PIPER

"Heading out?" Gloria's voice caught me on my way out of the office, which might have been the only building in all Castle Hollow right now that was properly decorated for Christmas—string lights everywhere, a big Christmas tree in the corner, fake snow and tinsel everywhere, garland strings and nutcrackers. Mostly, I'd just bought them with my own money and decorated the office myself, because if you want something done right, you know?

I hugged my laptop to my chest and turned back to where Gloria, a short and chubby woman around fifty years old with wild brown curls streaked with gray now, came out of the bathroom. I beamed at her. "I didn't know you were in today."

"I just got in a minute ago. And now you're leaving? It's like I did something wrong. I'm positively wounded, Piper. I think I'm going to cry."

Well, it wasn't like any of us got anything done in the office, which was why nobody cared that the head of the directory commission came in at noon. But to be fair, none of us got much done outside the office, either. It was a lot of busywork and pushing things off onto other people, and a lot of the time, I was the one things got pushed onto.

I'd been thinking a lot about what Lyra had said yesterday, about me being a pushover. Was it really being a pushover if you *wanted* to help people? If you *wanted* to help the town?

"Well, go ahead and cry it out, then," I said with a big smile. "You know me. I'm a wicked woman, I feed on tears."

"Better not give you the satisfaction, then." She put her hands on her hips. "So? How'd things go with Uptown Mikey yesterday? You put him in his place?"

"Um... I told him to shove a cactus up his ass? Does that count?"

She whistled low. "You're the sweetest little lady until you decide not to be, Piper. So, he's not coming around badgering us for sales anymore?"

"No, I, um... I think he's coming back soon." I put a hand on my hip. "Gloria, you never mentioned the tourism board is coming through."

Her smile faltered. "I, er, ah, well..." She forced a fake, nervous laugh. "Must have slipped my mind! Really thought you knew. Oh, well, yes, they, uh... they're coming on the twentieth."

"Why didn't you say anything? We're doomed if they see the way things are right now. The town center looks like a mothball's Christmas, and everybody's sad."

She threw her hands up. "Because we're all going to lose our jobs once that cultural grant folds, and I don't want to think about that. So... sue me if I want to bury my head in the sand!"

"We don't have to just lie down and accept it!" I said. "We can still turn things around, we can make things the way they used to be—impress the tourism board—"

"We probably *should* just accept Uptown Mikey's offer," she sighed. "Three point two isn't bad at all. The mayor would probably be happy."

"Gloria, are you listening to me?"

"I'm listening, but I think you're... well..." She wrung her hands. "Look, Piper, I love you, we all love you, but you are just a *little* naïve sometimes. And optimism is a good thing, but you're just a little bit... *too* optimistic sometimes. We've been trying for years to get this thing put back together. We won't do it in twenty days."

I huffed, turning back to the door. "Speak for yourself, Gloria. *I'm* doing what I can."

"Well, I think you're doing something hopeless, but I'll support you however I can. I think you're carrying half this town on your shoulders." She relaxed. "Where are you headed?"

I puffed my chest out, shoulders back. "I'm going out with the girl who moved in yesterday. I'll tell her you said hi. Thanks, Gloria."

I pushed out through the door before she could say anything else, out into the dreary cold of a town center that had long since lost its charm, everything dirty snow and sheer ice.

I was *not* letting it get me down, though.

Lyra was two minutes late, and she walked in importantly enough that it felt like I was in the wrong for expecting her two minutes earlier. *How* did people do that? I swear, no matter how much I tried, I could never pull that off.

"Sorry to keep you waiting," she said, sitting down across from me at the table by the window. Baron's Coffee was a charming little café overlooking the plaza at the town center, Christmas music playing over the speakers and cute little decorations in the thick windowsills and draped from the exposed rafters, but my attention was more on Lyra than anything else.

She had the most *amazing* kind of power in her whole demeanor—in the way she walked and talked, like she was important and never doubted it for a second. I didn't know that life. She was *really* pretty, which I bet could only help—she had dark hair she kept cut short, a deep brown like dark chocolate, with hazel eyes sharp enough to cut glass. Wearing a black blazer with chic, salmon-colored slacks, she looked professional without being pretentious, relaxed without being sloppy. I envied her in a million and sixteen different ways.

"Not a problem at all," I said, gesturing to the tray of croissants on the table. "Remember, I'm here as your official, um... welcomer, so you can do no wrong. Regular croissant, almond, and honey pistachio. I bet you'll love them all. Baron's knows what they're doing. And the medium roast you wanted."

"You didn't have to do this, you know. I just wanted to give you a break." She picked up the coffee and sipped gingerly at it.

I laughed nervously. "I don't really do the whole, um... breaks thing."

"It's delicious. Thanks, Piper." She relaxed. "So, tell me what all this on your mind with the committee is?"

"You can't get away with that," I laughed. "I'm here to welcome you, and I still don't know the first thing about you. What brings you to Castle Hollow?"

She didn't even falter. "My girlfriend broke up with me and spread rumors that I cheated on her, so I wanted to get away for a little while until my entire social circle stopped treating me like a hellbeast."

"Oh... um." I stiffened. "I am so sorry. That's terrible."

"She was the one cheating on me, but projection is a beautiful thing, isn't it?" She set her coffee down. "Mostly, I didn't want to spend Christmas there, so I picked a place said to have a nice small-town Christmas scene. Castle Hollow was at the top of the list. Not sure why."

I cleared my throat hard. "It has, um... fallen by the wayside a little bit."

She looked away. "I'm a contract writer, and I work remotely, more or less on my own schedule. So it doesn't really matter where I am. Most importantly, Castle Hollow doesn't have Sonia in it, and that's more than enough for me, Christmas celebrations be damned."

I looked down, cupping my hands around my peppermint mocha with extra whipped cream and crushed peppermint candy on top. "I think there's still hope for the Christmas celebrations."

She laughed. A second later, she cringed. "Oh. You were serious. That was a dick move."

"No, it's, um… it's fine. Everyone else laughs too." I sat up straighter. "The state tourism board is coming through on the twentieth. They haven't been here in years, and the Christmas celebrations here have really fallen off ever since Fredrik Walton left town, so… they're probably going to see the sorry state of things now and cut our cultural grant funding. So I kind of *have* to make a magical Christmas celebration happen here, if I want to keep my job."

She studied me, one eyebrow raised, just looking me over as she picked up her coffee and sipped lightly at it. Something about the way she looked at me gave me shivers. There was power in the way she did it, and it made me feel like she was ripping the mask off all my posturing and bravado without even saying anything.

"Frankly," she said, finally, "it sounds like you're doomed."

"I know why it would look like that, but… um… you know. I still have faith."

A smile flashed over her lips. I felt like I won a prize when I got her to smile. "You are... how do I put this? Quite a hopeless optimist, Piper."

I put a hand to my chest. "*Thank* you." I paused. "I think. Was that a compliment?"

"I think so. So, you're more of the Christmas committee right now."

I paused. "The Christmas committee? Do you think that can be a thing?"

"I think *you* could make that a thing. Just one look at you and I'm pretty sure you're all sleigh-bells-and-Santa-hats."

"I would *love* to be a part of the Christmas committee. Maybe I should float the idea to Gloria. Or just go over her head and ask Mayor Bolton. He'd probably go along with it for the laughs."

"You know, I wasn't suggesting you create a separate division for it. It sounds like your resources are stretched thin enough as it is, trying to put on a Christmas festival and fixing people's sinks at the same time."

I looked down. "Hey... what do you think could convince you to stay in Castle Hollow?"

"Stay?" She raised her eyebrows. "For how long?"

"Um... five years."

She let out a low whistle. "That's a tough one. A million dollars?"

"I think handing out a million dollars to every new resident would be expensive."

"You're really trying to turn this sorry place around, huh?" She shook her head. "You should be able to see they're just using you, Piper."

"I—look, I *know*." I pursed my lips, feeling my face flush. "But I care about this place. I care about the Christmases here. I was raised on them. And if they could happen once, they can happen again. I am *not* letting Uptown Mikey take over."

"Not letting—who?"

"Oh, right." I coughed into my hand. "Er... Mister Michael Landgrave, is what I mean to say. He wants to demolish the town center and build his row of McMansions along a four-lane stroad. I sat down with him for negotiations yesterday and told him to shove a cactus up his ass."

She choked on her coffee. "You told him to do what?"

"Shove a cactus up his ass."

She laughed, once, and then again, hanging her head as she laughed into her hand. "I don't know the man," she said. "But just from that, I'm already taking your side."

"Thank you. I really mean it. He's full of himself and annoying."

She shook her head, smiling. "I invited you here because I wanted to give you a chance to take a break, but... you really don't do breaks, do you?"

"That's what I said, and I stand by it." I sat up straighter. "Let it be known Piper Fairway does not give up or give in. Not for anyone. And I know you wanted to do me a favor, but... I'm your official welcomer. So I'm doing something for you. If there's anything I can do to make your time in Castle Hollow better, let me know. I'll go find your girlfriend and give her a stern talking-to, if you want. Maybe go around and clear up the rumors."

"Wouldn't that make me less likely to stay in Castle Hollow?"

I hung my head. "Oh my god, I'm so bad at this."

She laughed again, a big, bright smile on her features, and at least things couldn't be *that* bad, if she was smiling like that. She didn't seem like the type who went around smiling at everything and everyone, like some people at this table. "You really are... precious, huh, Piper? I feel like I need to wrap you up in a blanket and give you a cup of tea."

"Oh, like a cozy movie night or something? Get together in pajamas, wrap ourselves in blankets, drink some tea and watch a movie? I could do that. Tonight?"

She scrunched up her face. "That's not what I..." But she relaxed into a smile again, shaking her head. "You know? Sure thing. Sounds fun, I have nothing better to do, and I'm kind of invested in seeing you do something nice for yourself instead of just other people. Tonight."

"My place, then," I said, straightening my back. "I have a *really* cozy place I think you'll love. And, um... well, the house you're staying in kind of sucks, so you know."

"No arguments there. Sure thing, Piper. I'll text you."

I was *ecstatic*. If I could sell her on a cozy little movie night wrapped up in blankets, maybe I could sell her on helping me with the Christmas committee.

I think I was on to something.

Chapter 4
PIPER

I was feeling light like I wasn't used to on my way into the office the next morning, queueing up at the doors at 8:59 and waiting, phone in hand, for the moment it turned to 9 before I unlocked the door and stepped inside. Not that the precise timekeeping mattered much—nobody else was around.

I hummed a song to myself while I turned on the lights, including all the string lights, paused to shake a snow globe I'd put on Herman's desk, and set down the box of baked goodies I'd picked up from Baron's on my way into work. Nominally, I called out to the office, "Christmas breakfast!" just because it felt wrong to do it without telling everybody.

I'd barely gotten to my desk and set up my computer before somebody rang the visitor's side doorbell, and I wasn't really supposed to be on visitor-side duties, but, like... who else was going to take it? So I got up and hurried around the half-wall by Gloria's desk all stacked up with big red gift-wrapped packages, and I rattled with the door for a second to get it to open, coming face-to-face with my mom, who pulled me into a hug before I could even process that it was my mom.

"Honey, I just wanted to say I'm proud of you," she said, and I got a little melty and soft and squeezed her back. My mom had always been—um, spacey. I'd gotten my absentmindedness from somewhere, after all. But more than that, she'd always been sweet and supportive and keyed into every little thing I felt, and I didn't know how she'd heard about my work with the Christmas event, but I was so grateful I just wanted to burst.

"Thanks, Mom," I said, squeezing her tight. I got a faceful of her big red curls—as dramatic as my hair was, it was only a toned-down version of hers—and I breathed in deep and smelled the snickerdoodles she'd clearly been making this morning. Big surprise. I'd gotten my love of Christmas from somewhere, too, after all. "It's really hard and really scary and I don't know what I'm going to do if it doesn't work out—"

"Oh, sweetie." She stepped back from the hug, big blue eyes shining with that look she always had like she was looking right through me and at something else. My mom looked like she was about twenty years old. People mistook us for sisters all the time. "I love you so much no matter how it goes. Okay? Okay. So? When can you come visit home?"

"Oh, um, I'm pretty busy…"

She smiled wider. "I'm sure you are, Piper, sweetie. You work so hard. It's amazing. I know I could never work so hard at anything. You can bring Lyra, okay?"

That was exactly like my mom—someone got into Castle Hollow for about two seconds and she wanted them to come visit. I was impressed she'd already heard about Lyra in town. "I'm sure she'd love that," I said. "She's looking to meet people. I'll figure out when works for us! She can do afternoons, generally."

Her eyes sparkled as she took my hands and squeezed them. "I think you two will be wonderful."

Did she… know I was trying to get Lyra's help with the Christmas event? That I was looking for her to join the Christmas committee? My mom had always had a supernatural skill for gossip, but this was next level. I wasn't complaining though. I just beamed and said, "I really hope so. I think she's amazing."

"Oh, Piper, honey, I am just *so* proud of you." She pulled me into a hug again, squeezing the life out of me. "Okay, sweetie, I should probably get home. I have cookies in the oven."

I paused. "Um—Mom. Please go home right now. They're definitely ruined."

She tilted her head. "Do you think so? I went quick."

"No, Mom, they only bake for—please just go!" I pushed her out the door. "I love you so much, Mom! Thanks for coming to visit. Lyra and I will see you soon!"

Whitney was behind me when I closed the door, standing over the box of pastries—a woman in her late sixties with the most picture-perfect snow-white hair and comically large glasses, who had been bringing Christmas cheer into the office every day with her beautifully ugly sweaters. "You're always so sweet, Piper," she said. "The honey pistachio croissant is the perfect Christmas breakfast."

"I didn't hear you come in. Good morning, Whitney."

"I've got a stealthy streak. Used to be an assassin when I was your age. Took down political leaders in their sleep like it was nothing."

I laughed. "Sometimes, you say these things a little too seriously, Whitney. Will you be okay handling all the mail? There's a lot."

"Well, if I need help, I know where to find you."

Lyra's words hung around in my mind again, haunting me. Was I sacrificing my actual goals to let myself get suckered into helping everyone who wanted anything?

Last night with Lyra had been *so* much fun, and I felt like I was bouncing where I stood just thinking about when I'd see her again. She'd shown up in her sleek outfit from earlier but with a change of clothes ready, and I'd gotten the door for her in a bunny-printed onesie that made me feel a little bit outmatched next to her. Even after I'd insisted she get changed and she came out of the bathroom wearing a two-piece pajama set in a dusty rose color, she still felt way more put together than me, but I knew I had my brand and it worked.

"You do have a... cute house," she'd said, looking around the place. I got the coded message. She was admiring how much Christmas décor I had. We'd gotten hot drinks and sat in my living room together, on a big sofa with a red tartan blanket cover, next to a Christmas tree with every inch stuffed full of decorations, garland and string lights tied around the exposed rafters in my vaulted ceiling, nutcrackers lined up with scented Christmas candles that filled the place with cinnamon and sugar cookie aromas. Lyra looked like she fit in, settling back comfortably into the couch.

"Thanks. I love Christmas."

"I have picked up on that." She gave me a wry smile. "I've never been a fan, but your enthusiasm for it is... I want to say somewhat infectious."

I covered a laugh. "That's the goal. If I can infect everyone in Castle Hollow, then it's a win."

"It sounds dangerous when you put it like that."

"I'm nothing if not dangerous. Now, what's your favorite Christmas movie?"

She cleared her throat. "I have a longer list of blacklisted Christmas movies than I do favorites. My ex-girlfriend loved Christmas movies."

I squeezed my mug tighter, scowling into the void like her ex-girlfriend could see me. I wanted to give that woman a piece of my mind. Lyra was wonderful and deserved better. "If you don't want to watch Christmas movies, we can put on, like... a romcom or something! Oh, but... it might be a little straight for you. I'm just a boring old heterosexual."

She arched an eyebrow, a smile playing on her lips. "I'm bisexual. I won't recoil from a man kissing a woman."

"Okay! Cool." I gasped suddenly, sharply enough Lyra flinched. "Oh! We could put on *Love Actually*. What do you think? I've watched it a million times and I could make it a million and one."

She laughed into her hand, eyes twinkling, and I still felt like I was winning a great big prize every time I got that kind of look from her. "You really are a special person, aren't you, Piper?" she said. "I would love to."

"Oh my god, *yes*, I'm so excited," I said, as if the way I bounced to the TV remote didn't already say that.

We'd wrapped up in blankets and watched *Love Actually,* and then after a snack break we put on another movie, and by then Lyra was starting to fall asleep—she kept drifting on the couch next to me, and at one point she fell onto my shoulder and dozed off, and for some reason it just made me unbelievably happy. Just knowing I could give a new resident something so happy, so easy, so comfortable, that she could lie on me and breathe softly like this—even after everything she'd gone through before coming to Castle Hollow, she looked so at peace.

"I'm so sorry," she'd mumbled once she'd woken up, rubbing her eyes.

"You can sleep here. Even sharing a bed, it's probably way more comfortable than the bag of rocks I'm sure Beth left and called a bed."

"I won't impose," she mumbled, unraveling her blankets and standing up, but I'd latched onto her.

"No. Not allowed."

She looked back, eyebrows arched. "Leaving? Am I a prisoner now?"

"I'd make a terrible prison warden. If an inmate asked if they could leave, I'd probably say yes." I shook my head. "No! I mean, saying you're leaving just to not impose or something like that. If you don't want to sleep here, just say so. I won't be offended. But making up an excuse like *not imposing* when you know for a fact I would never in my life consider someone an imposition? That's banned. And the penalty is a thousand years in prison."

"A penalty I could escape by just asking to leave."

I laughed. "Yeah, probably. That takes the edge off a little."

She settled back into the couch. "You ever think maybe you *should* consider people impositions sometimes?"

"Um... maybe. But if I did, you wouldn't be near the top of the list. So, do you want to go home?"

She mulled it over before she shrugged. "Your place is nice. It's comfortable. I appreciate the offer."

"It's a sleepover, then." I picked up a pillow. "And a sleepover means a pillow fight."

"What—" She turned just to take a pillow in the face, the next word muffled into it, and when the pillow fell into her lap, she raised an eyebrow. "Are we in middle school now?"

"If middle schoolers do something that's fun, does that mean we can't do it too?"

She stared for a long time, and just when I'd expected her to make a remark about how childish I was, instead she moved at lightning speed and caught me off-guard with a pillow to the face. I squealed, falling back on the couch, and I snatched up my own pillow to defend myself valiantly from this transgressive attack that I absolutely, one hundred percent goaded on.

We'd gone to bed that night bright-eyed and tired out from laughing and throwing pillows, and Lyra had fallen asleep immediately. I'd lain next to her and just listened to the sound of her breathing, soft and slow, and I'd felt weirdly like this was how things should have been. The cadence of her breath, the warmth of her next to me, the way she smelled—sweet and fresh and crisp, like fresh linens and sweet peaches.

For all of my constant buddying up with everyone, I didn't get close like this with people very often—most people who'd stayed in Castle Hollow were older, with their own families and their partners and everything. I would have called them friends, but there was always something there—an odd weight to the friendship, a one-sidedness, an unspoken something that said we ran in different circles.

It wasn't fair Lyra was leaving. I didn't want to give this kind of friendship up. For the first time, I think I kind of resented Castle Hollow a little.

Maybe in a moment of spite or vengefulness against a world that only gave me so long like this with someone, I shifted closer to Lyra in the bed. She responded in her sleep, nestling against me and putting a hand over my side, and I relaxed against the blazing warmth that was Lyra under the sheets with me.

She'd apologized the next morning for being all over me when we woke up. "It's a little embarrassing," she mumbled while she was drinking the coffee I made her, looking away. "But I'm a bit cuddly in bed. I just hope I didn't say anything in my sleep."

"You talked about the magical rainbow pony you were riding..."

"Hello, projection. I hope you enjoyed the magical rainbow pony in your dreams."

I just laughed, happy to share a warm and cozy morning with somebody else in my kitchen as the snow drifted down against the window. "Don't worry about it. I'm cuddly asleep and awake. We should do this again sometime. As the head of the cultural committee, I can't let you go all alone."

"You're very committed to your job." She shook her head, tipping back her coffee. "I'd love to. Thanks for the hospitality, Piper."

It had kept me buoyed the whole way to the office, but now that she was back at her place doing her work and I was here doing mine, the reality of things settled in a little more, and I found myself looking at Whitney as she took the food she'd probably just assumed I'd bring in and told me about her plans to push her work off onto me, and I spoke like I was in a trance.

"I'm super sorry," I said, "but, um... I'm really busy with my stuff for the cultural committee, so

I can't handle anyone else's overflow work until like... at least after the twentieth."

It felt like I'd just confessed to murder, but Whitney just sighed. "Oh, fine. I'll find someone else to give it to. Maybe Herman."

I blinked. It had been *much* less of a reaction than I'd expected. "Um... well, good luck! I'm getting back to my work."

"Thanks for the croissant, Piper." She took it on a napkin and walked off towards her desk in the back, and I sat down at mine feeling a lot of strange feelings.

It morphed into a kind of wild optimism over the day—that maybe I *could* just set my own priorities, make my own schedule, and get the Christmas event handled after all—and by the time Gloria came in around noon, I'd already collated a budget for all the Christmas items to get the market stalls running next week. I came up to Gloria in a wild rush of excitement, but she met me in more excitement.

"Piper, you're a genius," she said, pulling me into a hug, and I squeaked.

"Um—thanks! What'd I do?"

"Lyra Simmons, that's what. Oh, I knew we were right to trust you." She stepped back from the hug and squeezed my shoulders, eyes shining. "How did you even know?"

"Um… I don't actually know anything."

Her smile only widened. "Really? That means I get to tell you?"

"I really hope you do, because I'm lost."

"Turns out Uptown Mikey is scared to death of her," she said, whispering too loud to be a whisper. "Her firm tears apart real estate sharks, represents a lot of renters' collectives against smug and awful landlords. He was on the phone with me, and he had a full freakout when I mentioned you were dating Lyra Simmons. I think we've got him on the back foot."

I paused. "Hold on. No, back up. Wait. When you mentioned *what?*"

"That you were going out with Lyra! I know it was just the one date so far, but I might have played it up a little bit so he'd be more scared…"

Oh my god. I'd said we were *going out.* I didn't mean it as a date. "I—Gloria—that's not—" I shook my head hard. "No, no, no, no. Oh my god, Gloria, we're not dating, we just went out for coffee! As friends! I'm straight!"

She waved me off. "Oh, you don't need to be shy here, Piper. We're all accepting and inclusive here. You know, I'd had a feeling for a while you would come out soon."

"I'm—there's nothing to come out of! I'm *straight!* As in I am a heterosexual woman who—" I shook my head. "Oh my god. Please don't tell me you told my mom."

"Well, I wouldn't be surprised if she heard about it. I got a little excited when you mentioned going out with Lyra."

Oh my *god.* She hadn't shown up to support me with the Christmas committee. She'd shown up to support me with my *girlfriend,* who, for the record, I did not have. She was proud of me coming out of the nonexistent closet. I was going to *scream.* How much time was I going to have to spend coming out as straight? Getting everyone to realize I *wasn't* dating Lyra?

"Gloria, oh my god. No, you have to fix this. I'm not dating Lyra. And—she's *very* lovely and I enjoy being around her very much, but I am completely straight. I mean, she's very beautiful and if I were gay then I'd probably be interested, but—I'm shooting myself in the foot saying that— um—"

"You don't need to be shy." She winked. "Gossip gets around quickly. Linda saw you two leaving your house together this morning, you know."

"Oh my god. It was a sleepover! We watched *Love Actually* and had a pillow fight—"

"You're both adults, Piper, you don't need to be coy about what you do in the privacy of your own home."

"I am not being coy!" I threw my hands in the air. "I am *strictly* attracted to men! I am a cisgender, heterosexual woman who—"

"I'd always wondered why you never got a boyfriend," she laughed. "You're so pretty and charming. Now it all makes sense."

"I never got a boyfriend because the only single guy my age around here is Jack Bender, and he smells like day-old meat!" I folded my arms. "I am *not* a lesbian, and I—"

"I get that you're shy, Piper—"

"I'm the exact opposite of shy!"

"—but think about it." She put her hands on my shoulders again. "This could save Christmas in Castle Hollow."

"How—what? Lesbianism? I'm not a lesbian. *She's* not a lesbian."

"Do you really think Uptown Mikey is going to sit back and let you throw a big happy festival?"

She shook her head. "Of course not. Why do you think the festival fell apart here in the first place?"

"Um... well. I mean, Fredrik Walton used to run it. He was our Father Christmas. Nobody really knew how to replace him."

She folded her arms. "You think he just got bored and left? Of course not. Landgrave offered him a job."

"I—what?"

"He works in one of his other offices now, over in Cleveland. I've been spending all night getting to the bottom of this, Piper, I'll have you know. Landgrave has had his eye on this place for a while."

She must have been serious, if she'd stopped calling him Uptown Mikey. "Are you saying he's been sabotaging Castle Hollow for years in some... deep conspiracy to buy out the town center?"

"Castle Hollow is in a prime location. With more of the tech sector migrating to the Midwest, there's a lot of talk about where the next hub is going to be. Seems like Landgrave's been in talks with someone from a big tech firm, and he's trying to capitalize on a new company park planned for the next few years a half-hour's drive from here."

I chewed my lip. "Meaning... he's not just trying to build along the town center, he's going to want to turn the whole town into strips of his tacky mansions."

"I know it sounds like a wild conspiracy, but it's not like it took a lot of effort on his part." She scowled. "Hiring Freddy already did a lot of damage. Putting up an ad campaign for one of his partners in a nearby city during our busy season just to draw people away, shifting his orders to our suppliers for buying season just so we can't get things—it's just been little things wearing us down. I'll bet he's the one who asked the tourism board to come through."

"So... you think he's going to ramp up the offensive now that we're only three weeks out."

"Not if we have your girlfriend in our corner." She put her hands on her hips, beaming now. "Lyra's the key to this. She's an old hand at putting down people like that, evil scheming real estate moguls."

"But I—um." I scratched my head. "The problem is that we're, you know... we're not girlfriends."

"Well, if you haven't made it official yet, that's fine, too—"

"There's nothing *unofficial!*"

She walked past me. "Oh, pastries. Piper, you're the best. I could kill for a glazed cruller right now."

Oh my god. This was a nightmare.

I really needed to talk to Lyra. About Mister Landgrave, of course, but also about the situation I'd gotten her into.

She was going to be so mad. I really hoped she wasn't going to yell at me.

Chapter 5
LYRA

I was starting to feel lucky I'd found a cute, absentminded redhead breaking my sink when I'd moved in. Out here now leaning against the ice rink, watching Piper hurry across the plaza towards me, dodging families with their kids streaming every which way, I admit I was still letting myself enjoy the view.

I knew checking out straight girls was a no-no, but there was something about Piper that was just so refreshing, and it drew my eye. Something about the spontaneity she would pull out while telling me to stay for a sleepover or starting a pillow fight—she was cute. And definitely attractive.

I was only here for a month. There was no harm enjoying the scenery. And that was all it had to be—just looking at pretty brown eyes and appreciating.

"Hi," she said breathlessly once she made her way up to me, her red tasseled scarf flapping in a cold breeze, fuzzy earmuffs almost buried in the wide waves of her hair. "Do you think the ice is in trouble?"

I paused. "I... hope not, since we intend to stand on it."

"Oh. What? No." She scrunched up her face. "Do you want to get on the ice? I think I'm in trouble. Are you upset?"

I put my hands up. "Easy, Piper. Breathe. What's up?"

She drew in a big breath, and let it all out at once in a big *puff* of air. "Nothing. I'm good. Okay. I'm cool. You might be mad, though. Let's get on the ice first so that I can focus on skating and not freak myself out."

"If it's going to stop you from having a hernia, I'm all for it."

She brought her own skates, so she waited by the edge of the rink for me to rent mine and join her, stepping onto the ice together. I wobbled a little bit—it wasn't like this was a common activity for me—but Piper glided like it was as easy as walking. She twirled around effortlessly and spoke to me while drifting backwards on the ice, her eyes anywhere but on mine.

"So... I mentioned Mister Landgrave before, right? How he wants to buy up Castle Hollow and build his tacky houses?"

"I remember, yes. Standard real estate douche."

"He knows you."

I fumbled a little, catching myself but swaying off balance. Effortlessly, Piper followed my path. "He knows me?"

"He knows your firm, at least. And enough about what you do in the firm. And, um... my boss Gloria told me that he's now afraid of us because you're around."

I just stared at her for a while. "Does he... know I'm not working for you?"

"No. Maybe? Um. This is the hard part." She cleared her throat. "Um... Gloria told him I'm your girlfriend."

She'd said it just as I was pushing against the ice to go a little faster, and I fumbled and fell. I came down hard on my butt, sliding across the ice with my momentum, and Piper skated around next to me and crouched.

"Are—are you okay?" She was paler than the ice right now. "I'm so sorry. That was terrible timing of me."

"I'm fine physically," I said, struggling to push myself back up on the slippery surface. Piper offered me her hands, and I took them, letting her help me up to my feet. She didn't budge no matter how much I wobbled against her. "Gloria told him what?"

She looked down, her marble-white turning to cherry-red. "Um... I told her yesterday that I was going out with you for coffee. Apparently she thought that meant I was taking you on a date, and she seems to have told the whole town—and Michael Landgrave—that I've come out as a lesbian and you're my girlfriend."

"I—don't know where to start with this. Just because we got coffee?"

She put her hands over her face. "Oh my god, I'm mortified."

Well, I could imagine that. I felt my head spinning, but even with that, it wasn't like I could get mad at Piper. Obviously it wasn't her fault. Seemed like she was just surrounded with a few... overexcitable friends.

"You don't need to be mortified over it," I sighed, rubbing my forehead. "It's not your fault, Piper. I'm guessing you tried your best to set the record straight."

She looked away. "Yeah, I did a terrible job. My mom came around congratulating me and I thought she was talking about me taking on the work for the Christmas event, but it turns out she was talking about me and my, uh, new girlfriend."

"Small towns really do gossip, huh?"

"Yeah. Especially Gloria." She wrung her hands. "I'm so sorry. I just wanted to give you a good welcome and make sure you weren't all alone."

I sighed. "This is what happens when you take on everything from everyone, you know. You don't need to do everybody's jobs. If you'd just—"

I fumbled, slipping when someone streaked past me quickly, and I reached out for the handlebars at the edge of the rink, but came up short—Piper caught me instead, and her hands steadied me, standing in front of me still skating effortlessly backwards, holding my hands and keeping me stable.

"See," she said, eyes lighting up, "I've actually been trying. Whitney told me I could handle her overflow work earlier, and I told her that no, I was going to be too busy through December to do that."

I paused. "Did you really?"

"Yep." She beamed. "She wasn't even mad! I was bracing myself to get in trouble and everything. Nice to know people want me around even if I'm not sacrificing for them."

I laughed. I wasn't sure why, just—there really was something special about Piper. Aside from the love of Christmas, she and Sonia were exact opposites—Sonia always putting on a mask, hiding what she really felt about things, trying to be better than everyone around her, and trying to prove to everyone that she was always right. Piper just smiled and laughed through things, saw an area she could improve in, went for it, and took it all with a cheerful attitude.

It was no wonder I'd felt like I was bouncing back easily from the breakup. Piper was healing, in a way. Spending the month around her didn't sound half bad.

"Look at you," I said. "You're doing great."

She laughed, flicking her hair back. "Thanks. I'm trying my best. Like, really, all the time, I'm just doing the very best I can."

"Well, doesn't sound too bad," I said. "Sounds like Landgrave will get off your case, then."

"Um—" She was right back to awkward, mumbling with a blush across her cheeks. "Yeah. That. Well, I mean, I guess so. But you're not actually working with us and we're definitely not dating—"

"We can change that."

"Oh!" She went somehow even redder. "Oh, wow, um. I mean, that's super flattering, and... you are *really* pretty, and if I were gay then I'd definitely... I mean, um... well, but I'm straight."

I fought down a smile. "What I meant, Piper, was that I could work with you."

"Oh. *Oh.* Oh, okay, well, that's mortifying. Um..." She turned away, leaning against the side of the rink, scratching her head and laughing. "Cool! Cool. Well, I'm just going to curl up in a corner and die of embarrassment."

Oh, she was *really* too precious. I leaned against the side of the rink with her, a smile playing on my lips. "Relax, Piper. I'm flattered I'd be your choice if you were gay."

"I was really hoping you'd just have somehow... not heard that." She gestured vaguely in the air.

"But I see why this matters to you now. It's clearly a lot more than just that you don't know how to say no to people. You want to save the town and you want to have a Christmas celebration like the ones that mean a lot to you. I don't like getting involved in things, but I'm kind of invested in this now. If there's something I can do to help with this Landgrave person, let me know."

"You really mean it?" She whipped her head over to me, beaming brilliantly. "You want to join the Christmas committee?"

"See, I don't remember going that far—"

"Don't worry! I can handle the lights and baubles. You can handle the legal expertise." She clasped her hands together. "Am I ever lucky for you, Lyra. Oh, but, um..." And just like that, she was back to mumbling awkwardness, looking down. "Well, if we're going to work together, they'll definitely think we're a couple."

"If it keeps the Landgrave creep at bay, let them."

She whipped her head back over to me, this time wide-eyed and lips tight. "Um—you mean that?"

"Being in a relationship with a woman isn't the most scandalous thing for me."

"Oh, um, but... well, I guess that makes sense."

I leaned back against the edge of the rink, fighting back a smile. "Besides, if Sonia finds out I'm already together with a pretty redhead who celebrates Christmas even better than she did, she'll be furious. And I love that."

"Um..." She looked down, wringing her hands at her waist. "I don't know if I'm that special."

"Please." Something about Piper being—well, Piper, made it easy to just say things. She was like alcohol on my inhibitions. "You're very pretty, and... refreshing to be around, in a lot of ways. I'd take you out if you weren't straight."

"Oh. Wow." She hunched her shoulders further, laughing nervously. I leaned against the edge of the rink with her, trying not to look like I was clutching desperately at the railing.

"Hope that's okay to say."

"It's more than okay. That's, um... I have low self-esteem sometimes, and it makes me feel a lot better about myself, so thank you."

I snorted. "You should see other people, if you think *you* have anything to have low self-esteem over."

"C'mon. Don't tease me. You'll make me blush."

"You have already been solidly blushing for the past ten minutes."

"I—look. Fine." She laughed, shaking her head. "Tease me all you like, then, I guess. What difference does it make? I'll just be dying."

There really was something about Piper. It felt like I was a different person when I was with her, and I was fast growing to like it. This might be a problem if I *did* catch feelings for her, but I was only here for a month. I'd live.

"So..." Her voice dropped to an awkward mumble. "Um... do you want to see my mom? She told me to bring you over sometime, and I said yes because I thought she just wanted to welcome you to town."

"What's your mom like?"

"Um... well, between me, her, Dad, and my sister, I'm the least absentminded and spacey."

I whistled. "Sure. Tonight?"

She laughed. "I like how readily you schedule things. I'm sure my mom would be happy to do tonight. I'll, um... help her make dinner so she doesn't burn anything."

"Sounds great. And we can talk about how we're... saving Christmas. Or what-have-you." I gestured to the rink. "Now, I get the feeling you're itching to show off how good you are at skating, so get on with it."

"Oh! Um... I wasn't, you know..."

I shoved her shoulder playfully. "It's good to be proud of the things you know you can do, Piper. I've been seeing how steady and comfortable you are on the ice, and I'm seeing people looking over at you waiting for you to skate. I want to see what you can do."

She ducked her head, blushing wider, but she smiled and nodded. "I, um... might have been hoping for a chance to show off. But don't tell anyone! That's unbecoming."

"My lips are sealed. Now, get out there. The judges are waiting."

She laughed, meeting my gaze with her eyes sparkling. "The judge is biased. She already thinks I'm pretty."

Well, Piper could play with fire a little. I just gave her a knowing smile as she took off, pushing away from the edges of the rink, picking up speed before she started on a long, slow turn in the center of the rink.

Wasn't like she was wrong. The judge did find her *quite* attractive, especially when she owned her abilities like this, pulling into a quick turn and coming out skating backwards, now the center of everyone's attention. And maybe going along with the pretend-couple agreement wasn't the best idea in the circumstances, but... I'd always been a self-indulgent person.

Chapter 6
LYRA

Piper's mom's house stood at the edge of town, tucked into the trees and right before where the plains jutted up into the cliffs surrounding the hollow. It was a gorgeous area that felt like the houses were one with nature, wild gardens off where the road carved winding paths through the trees, and dressed in a carpet of white right now, it was a place of serene silence I realized, distantly, I never would have found here in Castle Hollow without Piper.

I liked it. Maybe the girl was selling me on Castle Hollow. She did her work well in the cultural committee.

I followed my GPS onto a driveway and up to a house that might have disappeared into the foliage if it weren't snowy and dressed in Christmas lights right now—swathes of stonework blending in with the natural stone in the lot, wood construction like a storybook, especially with the string lights glowing against the snow. In the late evening light, the last traces of sunset fading orange and red through the snow-covered treetops, the house felt like a fairytale.

I hoped Piper didn't live with any wolves. I wouldn't put it past her.

I parked in front and stepped out of the car, huddling against the cold, and I walked around a lawn reindeer and up onto the stonework porch where a wreath hung on the door, mistletoe and candles nestled in its leaves. I rang the doorbell, and immediately I heard the commotion from inside, feet scrambling, people moving around and Piper's voice among others chattering. A second later, the door swung open, and a woman around Piper's age with the same red hair but bright blue eyes instead clasped her hands at her mouth at the sight of me, eyes sparkling.

"Oh my god," she said. "Oh, I just *knew* Piper would have good taste in women."

"I—excuse me?"

"You must be Lyra! Piper told me about how pretty you were. Oh, she's been waxing lyrical about you all day, Miss Lyra. Do you like ham and cheese sandwiches?"

"I... sure, yeah."

"Great." She beamed. "I forgot to defrost the turkey, so it's sandwich night."

From behind her, I caught a glimpse of Piper pushing through a room crowded with Christmas decorations, wearing a dress that faded from green to gold that, with her hair, made her look like Christmas made real. She really was stunningly gorgeous. It got a little upsetting that she could have low self-esteem.

"Mom, please don't tell me you're holding Lyra up in the doorway all day," she said, and I did a double take. The woman—who I could have sworn was maybe two years older than Piper—turned back to her with a laugh.

"Oh! I should let her in. I'm so rude. Lyra, please, come in."

She backed out of the doorway, and I stepped inside, scraping the snow off my boots. "So... you're... Piper's mom."

She straightened her back, beaming. "That's me! Louisa Fairway. It's *so* nice to meet you, Lyra. I just know you and Piper are perfect together. Oh!" She went wide-eyed. "Oh, I forgot I left the water running. Oh, I'll be right back."

She dashed off into the kitchen, and I heard pots and pans clattering. Piper, left alone in the living room with me, winced, but she turned back to me with a nervous smile, clasping her hands at her waist. "Well! That's that. Hi, Lyra."

"Hi. You look beautiful."

"Oh—thank you. You too." She laughed nervously. "Thank you for coming. It's, um..." Her expression faltered, and she dropped her voice. "I've never brought a date back to meet my parents, so... they're a little excited. They probably think we're going to get married soon."

"Not a lot of dating prospects out here, I guess."

She hung her head. "Nope. I mean, I never tried much. Even with people who have been here, I just... well, I never really connected with people. But let's not talk about that. Would you, um... care to join me for dinner?"

I offered her an arm. "I'd love to."

She slipped her arm under mine and shifted closer to me. "Great! Perfect. Um... I hope you don't mind lunch meat."

"I heard the story. Speaking of which... how old is your mom?"

She laughed awkwardly. "Forty-eight. I know. She doesn't look like it. Or act like it."

"I should check how old *you* are. Now I can't trust appearances."

"Twenty-five, thanks," she laughed. "You're..."

"Thirty."

"So I got myself an older girlfriend. Probably for the best. I want someone to show me the ropes."

That did not sound like a heterosexual thing to say. Piper was either not as straight as she claimed, or was a very good actor. If she wanted to experiment, I'd be more than happy to show her the ropes.

But I wasn't going to think about that while I was having dinner with her family.

We gathered around a mahogany table by a crackling fireplace, and *Let It Snow* played from an old record player that Piper's dad Charles kept as a treasured possession—he was a fifty-year-old man who actually looked his age, and so kind of looked like a creeper alongside Louisa, but he stayed quiet and just gazed at Louisa like she was the center of the universe while she rambled on about... nothing, really.

Sure enough, sandwiches were on the menu tonight, open-faced sandwiches on bread Piper had made herself. She served the bread and sat down next to me, shifting her chair closer, and I heard her let out this tiny, cute little giggle when I slipped a hand across her back, trying to look as obvious as I could. Louisa's eyes sparkled.

"You two are so sweet," she said. "I always had a feeling Piper would end up with a woman, you know."

"Um..." Piper stiffened. "Did you?"

"Didn't I, sweetheart?" Louisa said, looking back at Charles. He nodded.

"Of course, darling."

I thought it seemed quite nice to have a partner who, even after presumably decades of marriage, would still look at me like that and just dreamily say *of course, darling.*

Louisa looked back to me. "Ever since she was in high school and was just obsessed with Katie—"

"Mom, that was—" Piper scrunched up her face. "It wasn't like that! I just... liked her clothes."

Her parents exchanged a knowing smile. Piper's sister, Olive, maybe nineteen or twenty with their father's dark eyes and dark hair cut short, who hadn't looked up from her phone the whole time, just groaned.

"I miss when she didn't care about dating," she said. "She's been talking about Lyra this, Lyra that from the second she got back. I haven't been able to get in a nap all day."

"Olive, sweetie," Louisa said, "let your sister be happy. Coming out is a big deal. And Lyra is a wonderful girlfriend."

Olive rolled her eyes. Piper ducked her head, a flush across her cheeks, and I couldn't help a smile.

"Talking about me a lot, huh, dear?"

"I—um. Well. It's natural when I... you know... like you."

Funny, the way something in my chest responded to that like she actually meant it. I had a bad habit of that, though—however many times it was that Sonia had said something like that and I'd thought she'd actually meant it. Maybe I was just starved for affection.

"Well, it works," I said, and I leaned over and pressed a kiss against her cheek. "It happens I like you too."

She stiffened, and then laughed a nervous, wild laugh, wringing her hands under the table. "Great," she said, her voice too high-pitched. "Great, yeah, that's great. Very happy to hear that."

Kissing her cheek had probably been too much. Self-indulgence again. I'd back off and apologize to her later. Louisa, at least, didn't pick up on the mountains of nervousness and just beamed.

"I am so happy to welcome you to Castle Hollow. Piper told me about how you two are going to make the Christmas festival just like it used to be, and I was so proud I could have burst. I can't even organize my own morning routine. Just the other day I walked out the front door to get to work and my dear Charlie had to stop me because I'd forgotten to put on pants."

Charles just gazed at her lovingly. "It wasn't the first time. I'm used to it by now. I think it's cute."

I cleared my throat. "I'm... not as big on Christmas as Piper, but she's getting me to come around."

Piper elbowed me lightly. "Christmas always wins, you know."

"You know, Lyra, you should have seen it," Louisa said. "The festivals that Fredrik used to organize? You'd walk around feeling like it was so magical you might turn a corner and catch Santa Claus loading up his bag."

I wouldn't have put it past Louisa to still believe in Santa. I didn't press the matter. "Piper assures me it's a sight to behold."

"I'm sure you'll come around on Christmas when you—" Louisa stopped when a *thump* sounded from upstairs. Piper stiffened.

"Mom, what was that?"

"Oh, um... I don't know." Louisa beamed, going back to her food. "Well, probably nothing. What was I saying? It's like you could turn a corner and catch Santa—"

"No, Mom, it might not be nothing," Piper said. Olive groaned.

"Ugh, you're always so high-strung, Piper."

Charles sipped his wine, still gazing at Louisa. "If your mother says it's nothing, I'm sure it's nothing, sweetheart."

"No, it definitely *could* be something," Piper said. Another *thump* sounded, and she looked up. "See? It happened again."

"What did?" Louisa cocked her head.

"Oh my god, Mom."

I put a hand on Piper's back. "Hey, can you show me to the bathroom?"

Piper gave me the world's biggest *thank-you* look. "Of course! C'mon, I'm happy to show you around."

We slipped quickly out of the room, which immediately dissolved into talking about how cute a couple we were, and headed upstairs. Piper pushed open a door, leaning carefully into a small room that smelled a little like old wallpaper, and she relaxed.

"Oh, god. Just the Roomba. Mom must have turned it on without thinking about it again."

"Don't those things… generally avoid running into everything?"

She stepped inside the room, cluttered and with a Roomba that looked well and truly broken, driving slowly towards the wall. She crouched, picking it up and turning it off, with a sigh. "Yeah. It broke when my sister pushed it down the stairs. My mom keeps forgetting it's broken and turning it back on."

I scratched my head. "Your family's a bit… disorganized."

"You can say that again." She hung her head. "Thanks for, you know, getting me an excuse to come up here."

"It seemed like you needed a hand."

She cleared her throat, looking away. "Sorry I, um… freaked out and got a little awkward on you."

I shook my head. "No, I'm sorry. We should probably establish boundaries before we do—"

"No, no. I mean, yeah, we probably should, but I don't mind. You can do it again. Um…

assuming we're talking about the same thing. Are we talking about the same thing?" Her voice was getting high-pitched now, and she fussed with the tie at the waist of her dress.

"About me kissing you?"

"Yes. Yeah, okay, that's the thing." She laughed nervously, a little high-pitched and awkward. "Yes... yeah, that's okay. Just..."

I paused. "I can just not, you know."

"No, it's fine. Just... um." She hunched into herself so hard I think she might have shrunk out of existence. "Promise not to make fun of me?"

I arched my eyebrows. "I promise."

"I've, um... never... been kissed before."

I paused. "You're serious?"

"I am very, very serious. Um... it's not that I'm, like, some kind of unlikeable loser. I mean, sometimes I think I am, but it's just... you know. I've always been too busy to kiss people. And it always felt like a little bit of a commitment! And... um. I don't know. Not a lot of people I was ever interested in. So I thought I'd just... save it... for, you know, someone who really mattered a lot to me. But that's getting really, really awkward, because I'm twenty-five and, well, you know—I haven't had my first kiss, and this is the most embarrassing thing in the world, and I think I might just climb out the window and crawl into the snow and die?"

"That seems a bit excessive, Piper. It's not embarrassing." I cocked my head. "Just... surprising. I'd imagined you'd be popular. At the very least, in school."

"Oh, um... well, I had a couple boys who were interested in me." She laughed. "Derek Ball wrote me love notes and said I was as pretty as a canary."

"Is that—a compliment?"

"I'm not actually sure. It also raises questions. For example, does he want to kiss a canary? I hope not. He's married now to my mom's friend's daughter, and she doesn't seem to be a canary."

"A headscratcher, to be sure."

"But I wasn't interested in him. He wanted to be the world's greatest beatboxer. I have nothing against beatboxing! But he was certainly not on track to achieve his goal." She tented her fingers. "There was also Richard Browning, who wrote me a love note that started sweet, then veered into propositioning me, and then dovetailed into *way* too much disclosure about his pet play fetish. He said I would look good with a collar. I did not give him a reply."

"A—very wise move."

"Ryan Dolittle asked me out once. He was a cute guy who played basketball, and I supposed I didn't mind, so I went on a date. Picked me up and took me out to a nice restaurant, and I wasn't super feeling it but I wasn't totally put off, but then it really went off the rails when he said the waitress was an ugly bitch."

"So, you attract all the worst people."

She hung her head. "I suppose so."

I wondered if I should have taken that as an indictment. "You don't need to be nervous, Piper."

"Nervous? I'm not nervous. What makes you think I'm nervous?" She laughed, too high-pitched, and then forced a serious face. "I'm not nervous at all. What would there be to be nervous about?"

"Piper—"

"I'm not nervous. Really."

"It's okay to be nervous, too."

She put a hand to her head, sinking back against the wall. "Okay. I'm nervous."

"I'd guessed. That's okay. Want to tell me why?"

She took a long breath. "I feel like you're my only shot at saving this festival. I need to do this right. But when I start thinking about how I need to do something right, I freeze up. I don't want to lose you, Lyra." She made a face. "Um... that makes it sound like we're actually together."

I fought down a smile. "Relax, Piper. I'm not going to leave you. I'm serious about us."

"Oh my god, no, no," she said, waving her hands in front of her face. "Oh, god, I'll die. Um—no, but I guess I'm supposed to be able to keep up with that kind of thing. For appearances' sake. Okay. What's okay for me to do and say? We should set those boundaries now."

I shrugged. "Whatever you do isn't really going to bother me. Just ask before you grab any sensitive parts."

"I'm not going *that* far with the act. Oh my god. Can you imagine? My mother would probably..." She made a face. "Um... probably not really realize there was anything weird about doing that in front of her. That's gross to think about."

"I think what's more relevant is what *you're* okay with."

"Just no kisses on the lips, okay? I know I'm being silly, but you know..."

"It's not silly." It was precious more than anything else—the way she wanted to save it for someone important. Just like everything else, it was so refreshing. So Piper. I also hadn't been planning on it to begin with, so it wasn't like it was a problem. "Sounds good. Shall we head back down, then?"

I turned to the door, but she caught my hand and pulled me towards her. My heart jumped a little as she took both my hands, her eyes meeting mine, and she gave me a sweet smile.

"I'd go anywhere in the world if it's with you," she said, her voice dreamy, and suddenly this acting thing was a problem, because suddenly I *really* wanted to kiss her. She had the softest-looking lips.

She pursed those lips, and she looked away.

"S-sorry. I wanted to practice saying that kind of thing without breaking character, but I, um... I got embarrassed."

Yeah, me too. "Relax," I said. "Being a little embarrassed and nervous in places fits you well. I think you're doing just fine. Now, back to dinner?"

"Back to dinner." She smiled softly. "Hey, um... thanks. For being so patient and understanding. And for not making fun of me."

I laid a gentle hand on her arm. "Of course. You're perfect the way you are, Piper. And if we're being honest, I think it's cute that you decided to save your first kiss."

"Um—is it?" She went wide-eyed, blushing again. I wondered if she blushed a lot or if I was just good at getting that out of her.

"It is." I gave her a coy smile. "Whoever gets your first kiss is going to be lucky. I hope you know that. Let's get a move on."

"L-let's." I swear she stifled a giggle as I turned my back on her and headed back for the door, but it turned into an awkward noise as she turned back. "Oh! God, I plugged the Roomba in backwards. Hold on, hold on, hold on..."

Well, the apple didn't fall far from the tree.

Chapter 7

PIPER

I wasn't even late this time, stepping into the hotel lobby and out of the bitter driving cold of the wind. Rose looked up across the reception and beamed at me.

"Oh, Piper, you're here," she said. "Mister Landgrave is waiting for you."

"Thanks, Rose. Are you doing okay?" I paused. "Why the face today?"

She was smiling like the cat that got the canary. "So, when do I get to meet your girlfriend, sweetie?"

I had no idea how word had gotten around to her already. I put on a smile. "Oh! My girlfriend. Um... yeah! If you want to meet her, well... we're planning something at the community center soon. You should come catch us there. I'm trying to push her to include a dance."

"I always had a feeling you'd end up with a woman," Rose laughed, and I wanted to rip my hair out. *Why* did everyone in this town think I was a lesbian? I didn't *do* anything! "Well, tell Mister Landgrave hi for me. Good luck with the meeting, okay?"

I puffed my chest out as I headed past her and into the room where, just like before, Michael Landgrave was on his phone. This time, channeling all the confidence I felt like I would have if I were more like Lyra, I walked around to his side of the table and pulled the phone from his hand, hitting the End Call button. He looked up at me slack-jawed.

"Our meeting time is now," I said. "If you're trying to make a deal, you could learn some manners and not insult the person you're making a deal with by hanging out on the phone with your boyfriend."

He snatched the phone back. "I asked to meet Bolton, and specifically that I didn't want to see you again. Why you again?"

Suddenly I was the most powerful person in the world. I sat down, folding my arms, and I reveled in his expression. "Mister Landgrave, if I didn't know any better, I'd say you're afraid of the girl who's dating a lawyer."

He huffed, drawing himself up to his full height. "Lyra Simmons is no lawyer. I took the liberty of looking into your... girlfriend. She's a contract writer who barely scraped through law school."

"Even more interesting that you're so afraid of her, then," I said. "Is it because she's better at getting women than you are?"

He turned his nose up, going red. "I *asked* to see Bolton. I'm leaving."

"I sure hope so! I've been waiting all day to hear you say something nice like that. By the way, I just wanted to let you know, you're not going to intimidate us. Tell Fredrik Walton we're going to make an even better Christmas event than he ever did."

He shoved away from the table and stood up, marching towards the door. "You and your friends are going to regret this," he muttered.

"You sound like a cartoon villain. Go shove a second cactus up your ass and see if it can wedge the first one any further up there!"

He slammed the door shut behind him, and I collapsed back in my seat. After a second, I put a hand to my chest and laughed.

"That was pretty good," I said. "Phone snatch? A shot at Fredrik? The second cactus up the ass? I am good."

"I'm back, Christmas Committee," I said, bursting into the room with a box of cupcakes, and Lyra looked up from her laptop, sitting at a desk with Gloria, Whitney, and Beck, who only came in to help on Saturdays with his mad-scientist hair and coke-bottle glasses, all clustering around her. "Oh. You're popular."

"I still never agreed to be Christmas Committee," Lyra said, and Gloria put a hand on her shoulder.

"Lyra, be good and listen to your girlfriend. She's a smart one."

I think I got the idea now of why they were clustering around her. Lyra had only come into the office an hour ago, and it was the first time my coworkers had met her, so... well, odds were, Gloria wanted to gossip about our relationship, Whitney wanted an excuse to not work, and Beck—um—I had no idea. He just did his own thing.

Lyra stood up with a sigh, reaching across the desk and giving me a sweet smile as she took the cupcakes. "Thanks, angel," she said. "You didn't have to do this, you know."

Gloria positively *squealed,* elbowing Whitney. "She calls her *angel,*" she said.

I got a weird little fuzzy feeling all of a sudden, and I forgot how words worked. "Uh—I-I know. Just... wanted to do it for you, s-sugar... squish."

I had no idea in what universe *sugarsquish* was a pet name. I'd just blanked. The smile playing on Lyra's lips said she didn't mind. "How'd the meeting go?"

"Mm. I told him to shove a second cactus up his ass and see if it could wedge the first one any further up."

She opened the box and set out traying up the cupcakes. "I would have expected nothing less from you, Piper. I put together some plans for the community center event," she said, glancing back at her crowd of admirers, "that these people have been oohing and aahing over. I'm mostly concerned with what you think, though. Want to give it a look while we pick up some coffee together?"

"Oh, um—if you want coffee, I can just go—"

She came around the desk, took my hand, and like she'd just stepped out of a dream, lifted it up to her lips and kissed my knuckles. My mind fizzled like I'd lost reception. "I'm using it as an excuse to get some time together, darling."

Gloria all but screamed. My brain melted. I forgot how to speak English. Whitney stole a cupcake. "You're so... dreamy," I laughed nervously. "Okay! Let's... let's go. Before Whitney eats all the cupcakes."

Lyra snapped back at her. "Whitney! Those are for our end-of-week party. Piper went to the trouble of getting them for us. Don't disrupt her plans."

Lyra was the strongest person in the universe, because Whitney put the cupcake back down. "Sorry, Piper," she laughed. "Your girlfriend's too quick on the draw. I've lost my stealth edge."

I still felt a little... mushy and weird as we headed out back, our boots crunching in the snow, and as I led the way to the coffee shop.

There was something nice about having my people all excited about my relationship, talking about how cute we were. I... wondered if I was missing out on a big part of life. It felt like it filled some space I'd been waiting to have filled.

"Thanks again for picking up snacks," Lyra said, walking close by my side as the smell of the wintry air filled my nostrils. "You know you don't have to do things for me all the time."

"I know. I just like to. It's my love language."

She winked at me. "Thanks, sugarsquish."

"Oh my god. Can we pretend that didn't happen?"

"Probably not. We had a crowd of your coworkers who were, as far as I can tell, making notes of our pet names."

I buried my face in my hands. "Oh my god. And one was *Gloria,* so she's going to tell everyone I've ever known about how I'm a lesbian who's dating a hot lawyer from out of town and how I call her *sugarsquish* and how that means I'm probably a bottom."

She made a face. "Would Gloria gossip about whether you're a top or—"

"She would one hundred percent gossip about whether I'm a top or a bottom."

"I'm not going to approach that thought. Also, I'm not technically a lawyer, you know."

"You graduated law school and you draft legal documents. If that's not a lawyer, then I don't know what is." I turned down a side path, taking the steps carefully down—the sheer ice over them still made things scary at best. "How'd you end up going to law school, anyway?"

"Same as everyone else. Combination of watching too many legal dramas growing up, and my parents wanting me to make a lot of money. Then I realized law is a lot more boring than in the dramas, and my parents wouldn't talk to me anymore after I started dating a woman, so none of that held up anyway, but I like contract writing. It's like solving puzzles."

"I'm... really sorry about your parents."

She waved me off, but I saw the stiffness in her expression. "Don't worry about it. I hadn't exactly been psyched about going back for Thanksgiving dinners anyway. Sorry, my backstory's not very interesting. Let's talk about the plans. I've been finding people and charting out what's possible in our limited timeframe, and I think we can make the dance and the festival happen, but I feel like if we're trying to impress the tourism board, we'd be better off putting all our resources into the thing they'll see."

I shook my head. "Denied."

"Ah, that was strict. Mind explaining why?"

I grinned. "Because! Christmas magic is in your heart."

"Hm. So we need surgery to get it out?"

"Very funny, sugarsquish." I elbowed her as we turned the corner and up to the empty plaza in front of the coffee shop, dirty windows and bare decorations. "No amount of spending on the festival is going to make it magical if the townspeople aren't excited about it. The dance is a critical component of the magic, because it's our shot at making the people of Castle Hollow believe in Christmas magic again. If and only if we can do that, then the festival will be a success."

She grinned. "You know I did my undergraduate in math?"

I paused with my hand on the doorhandle for the coffee shop. "I didn't, but that's really cool. I always liked geometry, but somehow I don't think that's the same thing. How's that relevant?"

"Makes a girl swoon when someone uses *if and only if* correctly in a sentence." She winked before she headed into the building, and I stood there blankly staring at the space she'd just been, trying to figure out why I got all weird and squishy inside.

I swear I'd been feeling *weird* ever since she, um... technically gave me my first kiss. I mean, it was only on the cheek, but it had felt like a lot in the moment.

I was going to squeeze *if and only if* into half my sentences. If only because I felt like I won a prize every time I made her smile.

"Coming, darling?"

"Oh!" I shook my head, realizing Lyra was standing inside the doorway looking back at me. "Sorry, sorry. Spaced out."

"Something new for you."

"Yeah. I mean, no, not really. I'm getting the coffee traveler for the office, but I'm also getting a peppermint mocha, because I deserve it. If you want something, it's on me."

She smiled wider. "It's on *me*. Your peppermint mocha. I already called ahead."

"You did—*what?*" I whirled on her, but sure enough, Ethan behind the counter grinned and set down a big peppermint mocha with extra whipped cream and crushed peppermint candies on top, along with the coffee traveler. "Oh my god. Lyra! I was going to—when did you even—how did you even know what I wanted?"

Ethan was the one who answered. "I told her you always get the peppermint mocha. I'm happy to see you're finally with someone, Piper. I always thought you'd end up with a woman."

I swear to god. I forced a smile. "Yep... you're not the only one!"

"Thanks so much," Lyra said, picking up the coffee traveler. "Coming to the community center event?"

Ethan, who was a scraggly kind of guy in his late thirties and always wore a printed button-up—maple leaves were the print of the day today, which was odd for a snowy winter's day, but I wasn't questioning it—scratched his head. "I've heard some talk about it, but I don't know. Are there going to be drinks?"

"Of course," I said, lighting up like a Christmas tree. "Eggnog, mulled cider, mulled wine—"

"Hot chocolate," Lyra said. "The girlfriend insisted on it."

I puffed out my cheeks. "It's Christmas, Lyra! How can you have Christmas without hot chocolate?"

Ethan chewed his lip, wiping down the counter. "I'll see if the wife wants to go. The last few Christmas parties around here have been a bust. I think maybe people just want a quiet Christmas."

I leaned over the counter, giving him my best puppy-dog eyes. "*Please*, Ethan? It would mean the whole entire world to me. I'd be so, so happy if you came."

He scrunched up his face. "Er, well... I guess we can try to make it."

Lyra waited until we were back outside to laugh. "Played him like a fiddle," she said. I sipped my drink, pure happiness in a cup.

"I've been told I look like a kicked puppy sometimes. Might as well use it in our favor."

"Touché. All right, Piper. I think I see your logic. A Christmas dance at the community center. If it fails, at least we'll know where we stand with the festival."

I laughed. "Fails? I don't even know the meaning of the word, Lyra. We're going to save this sad, sorry little town."

Chapter 8

LYRA

Piper took me out a lot over the next week. For the most part, I was just along for the ride.

It started the day after our end-of-week office party, where I'd sat by Piper's side and put a hand on her back while the rest of the town hall employees—a skeleton crew to put it kindly— laughed and gossiped over cupcakes and coffee, and titillated about me and Piper, about the Christmas event next week. I'd woken up the next morning, in my cold and hard-as-rocks bed at my rental house, to a text from Piper.

If I tell you you're banned from working Sunday mornings, will you come over and help me bake gingerbread cookies?

I laughed, huddling against the cold in the drafty old bedroom that was so bad I swear I could have seen my breath. I could just hear the text in Piper's voice. *Can we negotiate? Half an hour of email time, and then all the cookies you like.*

Nope! You can take your emails here while the cookies are baking. I have a surprise for you.

"Well, if there's a surprise," I said, even knowing full well I wouldn't have been able to dispute Piper for long. It wasn't like I didn't want an invite.

The sun was still just rising when I got to Piper's house, not far from the town center, at the top of a hill and with a gorgeous view over where the plain dipped into a frozen lake at the center of the hollow, cozy houses peppered here and there across the landscape. The low-angled sunlight gleamed like gold off the sheeny snow surface around her house—which looked positively like a gingerbread house, with its Christmas decorations and lights in all the windows—and I breathed in the cold air and the smell of sweet spices as I knocked on the front door. Piper opened the door in a nightrobe, messy hair and no makeup, and I'd be lying if I said I didn't like the view.

"You're here," she laughed, eyes bright.

"You say that as if I might not have been."

"You never know. Maybe you sneaked off to do some illicit emails." She turned to the side and came back a second later with a small gift-wrapped package, crisp red wrapping paper and a big bow on top. She thrust it out towards me. "Ta-da! It's your surprise. Open it."

"I... love it, but any chance I can come in first?"

She blinked. "I'm going to be honest, Lyra, I kind of forgot we were in the doorway."

The present waited until I was inside, boots and coat stripped off by the front door and the two of us sitting on her couch. Piper leaned on me, squishing into my side and looking intently at the package as I cradled it in my hands, and I honestly wasn't sure where she got off being this cuddly and affectionate. She was feeling more like a girlfriend than Sonia ever did.

"The packaging is so pretty, I'd hate to ruin it."

"Pretty things are meant to be destroyed."

"A very violent sentiment coming from you, Piper." I tore the paper neatly at one corner, pulling out a small jewelry box. My heart skipped a beat as I caressed the soft velvet of the box. "Piper. You didn't get me something expensive, did you?"

"Nope. Fished it out of the bargain bin, *damaged and unwanted* section, ninety-nine percent off. I paid for it with two nickels and a bubblegum wrapper from my coat pocket." She shoved me. "Just open it! I think they'll look cute on you."

I opened the box and found a pair of earrings inside, small and elegant drop earrings that had a spiral-shaped crystal set in each. Piper ducked her head bashfully.

"I'm sure you're used to nicer quality stuff, but... this made me think of you."

"It's gorgeous," I said quietly, holding them up to the light. "You didn't need to do this. Thank you..."

"It said the crystal is shaped in accordance with the golden ratio. I don't have the first clue what that means, but it sounded mathematical."

I lifted one of the earrings out of the box and held it up to the light, the cut shape of the crystal gleaming. She was right—it curled in the distinctive nautilus swirl shape, only noticeable on close inspection, tastefully done. I shook my head. "You only knew since yesterday afternoon that I studied math, and you already got me a gorgeous gift suited for it."

She laughed, puffing her chest out a little. "I think I'm a pretty good gift-giver. It's one of my skills in life."

Honestly, it... messed with me a little. I'd always considered relationships a low priority. Something not to be avoided if it happened naturally, but not something worth seeking out. Getting together with Sonia had just—presented itself one day, and I took it. Getting out had been sort of a relief. I'd convinced myself relationships were all like that, and people just built them up too much, put too much importance in that whole thing.

But when I thought about the person who would one day get to date Piper, I was jealous.

"I think," I said, putting the box down, "I'll be wearing these to the dance. And if anyone asks, I'll just tell them my beautiful sugarsquish got them for me."

She buried her face in her hands. "Oh my god. How long am I going to suffer with that one? I'm so embarrassed."

Well, only through the rest of the month. But I didn't want to think about that. I was enjoying the here and now with Piper. Overthinking it would ruin it.

"You're cute, and it suits you, in a way." I squeezed her shoulder. "Now, I hear I have to make gingerbread cookies before I'm allowed to get on my emails."

"You shouldn't have to get on them on a Sunday morning anyway!" But she beamed, standing up and offering me a hand. "But if you *must*, then yes, you have to earn it by paying the cookie tax. C'mon, I'm starving for cookies."

We made cookies. And honestly, it was kind of fun, measuring out spices and making batches in the mixing bowl. Piper laughed big and bright and loud the whole time, and I got caught up in her rhythm and couldn't even complain when she put on *Have a Holly Jolly Christmas*.

When I asked her why we were making six batches of cookies, the only answer she would give me was *bribes*. I didn't press the matter, because there was no getting something out of Piper unless she decided to share it, so I just helped with the cookies until we got to sit down with breakfast, the last cookies in the oven. I went back to my work emails once she'd gone to take a shower, and I was in such an obnoxious uplifted Christmas spirit, I didn't even turn off her Christmas music.

I didn't get far before I knitted my brow, frowning at an email from my department head Mr. Sanders. *There have been three different external inquiries into you in the past twenty-four hours*, it said. *They've all been general queries, and I haven't been able to find out why people are so concerned about you all of a sudden. I looked over your files and nothing stands out. Any idea why you're suddenly a lightning rod?*

Well, if my keen instinct for pushy men wasn't mistaken, that had to be Uptown Mikey. If all he was doing was general inquiries, he was as impotent as he sounded, but it didn't hurt to play on the safe side. *Odds are it's Michael Landgrave from Landgrave Estates. Strongarm investor in the developing plains. I've made friends recently with someone he's trying to intimidate. I don't think he'll escalate, but if this continues, we may have to shut down communications with his team.*

By the time I finished the rest of my emails, Mr. Sanders had replied. *We're already sticking our necks out in a lot of places, Simmons. You know your contracts don't let you just pick up jobs with whoever you like. Don't get us in trouble.*

I frowned. Mr. Sanders was normally unflappable. I had to wonder why he was so worried about a few cold inquiries. *I'm not doing any legal work for my friend. I'm doing a few favors at most. I'm not picking fights with real estate moguls.*

But it still bothered me even after I'd closed my laptop and Piper came back in the room, hair still slightly damp, wearing a puffy blouse and a jacket. She leaned over the counter, beaming at me.

"Still listening to the Christmas music," she said. "The Grinch's heart has grown three sizes."

"I guess so," I laughed, trying not to sound bothered with Mr. Sanders' email on my mind. "You're ready to go out. Where are we headed? Bribing people?"

"Bingo. First up is my old next-door neighbor Bella Burnes. B Squared is going to be easy to convince to attend the dance, so we only need to bring her a few cookies and presents as bribes."

"Ah, and now the secret plan comes together."

She winked. "I thought it'd be nice to introduce you to everyone in town, too. I mean, they already *know* you—gossip travels fast—so might as well make the introductions. All part of my official duties as the head of the cultural committee to welcome you to Castle Hollow."

"Doing me a favor and doing the town a favor by doing as many people a favor as you can. Seems you'll do something nice for everyone but yourself."

She scoffed, waving me off. "Please. I get to take you out places and talk to all my friends together with you. And I'll snack on gingerbread cookies the whole time. Win-win-win. Just help me decorate them first? I'll give you my best puppy-dog eyes."

Oh, she already had me wrapped around her little finger. She didn't need the puppy-dog eyes.

We decorated the cookies together, laughing over the wild faces she made on hers, or the amount of detail I put into mine—which only seemed to me like a reasonable amount of detail for a gift—and we packed up and headed out before long. Bella Burnes lived near Piper's parents' house, in a house that looked like a storybook cottage, and she met us at the door—a tall, noodly sort of woman with big, frazzled hair, who threw her arms out wide for Piper.

"Piper! It's been forever since I last saw you."

"I know! I mean, it's been a week, but... it's been forever!"

"It's been forever since I last saw you not canvasing for work or something like it," Bella said, and she looked at me. "And this is the girlfriend I've heard so much about? She's awfully pretty. You know, your mom always said she was sure you'd marry a woman one day. I always saw the logic in it."

Piper let out a long-suffering sigh. I really wasn't sure why everyone and their dog thought Piper was a lesbian, but I wasn't reading into it. "Yep... well, lucky me I scored the best one," she said with a dry laugh. "So! We've come to try convincing you to join us for the dance next week at the community center, and I know—"

"Oh, sweetie, I'd love to, but I have my gardening club meeting—"

"—that you have your gardening club meeting, but it *is* December and everything is covered in snow, and you're just meeting the gardening club to hang out and have drinks." She clasped her hands together. "Which you can do at the dance, too. *And* there will be eggnog."

Piper was a master negotiator. Bella chewed her lip, casting her gaze skyward. "Well, if you put it like that..."

"But," Piper said, straightening her back, "I know I have to bribe you before I can convince you! So I brought gingerbread cookies. Do you want to sit down together and share some? I wanted you to meet my... uh, my girlfriend anyway."

Piper had Bella eating from her hand. Only a few minutes later, we were gathered around the older woman's kitchen table, a cluttered disaster that she pushed things around on to make us a space to sit and eat, and we talked together like we were all old friends. When I mentioned my work, Bella lit up and said her nephew had gone to the same law school—a public attorney now who worked far too many hours for far too little pay, and I commiserated on my legal internships. Before long, like gingerbread cookies and hot chocolate loosened tongues faster than any alcohol, her expression had grown heavier and she'd admitted how hard and lonely it had gotten for her since her husband passed last year.

"You don't realize how much you build your life up around one person until they disappear," she said, her voice hollow. "You two be good to one another and enjoy the time you've got, you hear?"

Piper looked down. "Um... y-yeah."

Something possessed me to reach across the table and put a hand down on Bella's. "I'm really sorry for your loss," I said. "I can't imagine how much it must still hurt. But I think I've been finding it's never too late to meet a community for the first time all over again."

Her eyes shone, and she smiled, but when she opened her mouth to speak, she just started bawling, instead. Piper shot to her feet.

"Uh-oh. Emergency hug. Lyra, help."

We gave Bella an emergency hug. By the time she was able to speak again, she wiped her eyes and spoke shakily.

"Getting out to the dance will be good for me," she said. "You found a good girlfriend, Piper. I'm really happy for you both. Oh, I need another cookie."

And even though I didn't want to be corny, I walked out of the house later feeling like I had another friend in Castle Hollow. Piper nudged my shoulder as we walked through snowed-over garden plots back to the car. "That's one person for the dance."

"Who's next on the agenda?"

She beamed. "I am so glad you asked."

We went to visit three other people in total, and when we got back to Piper's house, I crashed hard. Piper laughed when she found me slumped over the couch.

"Tired?"

"I'm not as extroverted as you are."

She dropped down next to me, a hand on my back. "You did great, though. I couldn't have gotten everyone on board without you. Thanks for coming along."

"I think I've had enough gingerbread for the rest of the year now."

"Don't worry. Tomorrow will be sugar cookies."

"Tomorrow—do you ever rest?"

She laughed. "Do you have to ask? There's no rest for the wicked, Lyra, and no one is more wicked than me. Don't worry. I know you're working tomorrow morning, so I can make the cookies. But, um..." And suddenly she was bashful again, looking away. "If you want to save some time and effort, you can just stay here tonight. You look way too tired to go back and sleep at that awful house."

I really needed to say no at some point. Otherwise this little crush I had on Piper was going to be a problem. But I'd always been a self-indulgent person. "I'd love that," I said.

"Great. Me too. I never got to have sleepovers when I was a kid, and I need to make up for it now—"

I hit her with a pillow. She laughed, falling backwards on the couch, and it took zero time for us to launch into another pillow fight, before we collapsed laughing on the floor.

I didn't know what had gotten into me. But I was having fun. And falling asleep next to her that night, feeling the way she shifted close to me— that sweet smell of cinnamon and ginger on her— I was liking a lot of this.

But damn if I couldn't feel her heat blazing under the sheets next to me and sending my mind off in the wrong directions.

The next day didn't look too different—work in the morning, and thankfully no interruptions from Landgrave, on my laptop sitting on Piper's couch listening to her hum to herself while she made cookies. She left for the office eventually, telling me to make myself comfortable, and I was just finishing up my work when she got back. We made another cookie tour together, and she glowed talking about how all the staff she gathered for the event seemed to be catching the enthusiasm.

And again, I crashed hard once we got back to her place, and she didn't even have to offer this time. We both went through the motions of getting ready for bed together, and by now we even had a clear division of which side of the bed was hers and which was mine.

And again, I found myself thinking all the wrong things as I was lying next to her.

Catching feelings for straight girls was the worst.

Chapter 9
PIPER

Gloria gave me a tight squeeze. I let out a grunt, but I squeezed her back. After a solid six or seven seconds, I said, "Um... hey, Gloria. Any reason I'm getting squished right now?"

"I've been hearing so many people talking about the dance tomorrow. You and your girlfriend are geniuses. I'm so glad you were able to seduce a sexy lawyer."

"I—um. Yeah, me too." I fussed in her bear hug. The rest of the office was clearing out, five o'clock now and nobody stayed late. I used to be the exception, but Lyra had made it clear I was to stop letting myself get used all the time. And... besides, I wanted to go home and see her again.

"I'm starting to wonder if maybe you're right," she said, finally stepping back from the hug. "Maybe there *is* still some hope for Christmas in a sad, miserable little backwater slum of a town like this one."

"That's a pretty harsh judgement, Gloria."

"Oh, I just say that because I love the place." She shook her head. "But really, you have to admit, it's been pretty depressing since Freddy left. Your girlfriend really was the key ingredient." She squeezed my shoulders. "I can't wait to see you two at the dance tomorrow. You're going to be the belles of the ball, you know."

"Oh! Um. Right. I guess we'll be dancing together." I laughed nervously. The thought of dancing with Lyra in the middle of the community center, the whole town gathered around us—it kind of gave me a nervous tumbling in my stomach. "I forgot I'd be, um... at the dance, too, I guess."

"Oh, so you haven't been practicing your dance?" She tutted. "Better go home and ask your love to dance with you deep into the night."

"You know, saying things like that, um... you know we've only been seeing each other for ten days now, right?"

"Love is love. You just know when it hits you." She waved me off. "You know... I was worrying about you for a while."

"Because I was just... clearly such a closeted lesbian?"

"Well, of course." She folded her arms. "Something like that. Just... you didn't seem to have any personal life, you know? Most of the people your age all moved out of Castle Hollow. I'm not saying I wish you had, because I'm glad you're here, but... oh, sweetie, you know how it is. You've got to be young when you're young. You've got to stay out too late with your friends, quit your day job to be in a band that won't last for a week, fall in love with the wrong person and love the mess. You've been so grown-up, working so hard at a nice, steady job and looking after everyone. I worried you were going to look back and realize you did all your grownup living while you were young, instead of saving it for when you were grown up."

I don't know why, but it felt like she'd just hit me over the head with a spade. I blinked fast. "I... are you telling me I should be more immature?"

"Well, of course! You're still just a kid, Piper. When else are you going to be immature?"

I scratched my head. "I... but. What's wrong with just doing things the right way?"

"Because you spend so much time trying to find out the right way to live that you figure it out, get it all settled and ready to start living, look up at the clock, and realize it's already time for bed, that's why." She patted my shoulder. "That's why I'll look the other way if you get blackout drunk tomorrow and dance on the counters. We'll pick up after you, for a change, and you can get back to your responsible living."

I felt like she'd just reached into my chest and yanked my heart out. Suddenly I could feel an aching emptiness there where there was definitely supposed to be something, and I chewed my lip. "I'll, um… well, I don't really like alcohol much, so I'll just drink way too much hot chocolate."

"That's a good start, sweetie. That's a good start. Go make the wrong choice every now and then. It's the most liberating thing you can do. Speaking of making the wrong choice, I'm going to get takeout from three different places for dinner tonight, and I'm going to love it until the morning."

I stood there in the hallway watching as she left, until it was just me, standing in the dim lights of the office, my hands clasped at my waist. I breathed in deep, closed my eyes, and let it out slow.

"Okay," I said. "I can do that. More bad choices, Piper. You've got this."

Lyra was brewing coffee when I came into the house, and she turned back and smiled at me.

"Hey," she said. "You've got a look like a girl on a mission."

"Kiss me."

She blinked. I did too.

"I—was hoping actually to work my way up to that with a little more preamble and stuff, I guess." I scratched my head. "I mean, if you want to."

"What?"

"The—dance—tomorrow." I'd had some gusto a minute ago. Now I wasn't sure where it had gone. "I mean, everyone's going to be looking at us! And... um... expecting us to do coupley things. So I just think it'll be weird if we don't... kiss..." My voice fell off to a mumble, looking down at the floor. Lyra stepped away from the coffee pot, coming over and putting a hand on my arm.

"Hey, Piper. We don't have to do anything you're not comfortable with. We can play it off any number of ways. We'll say you're shy and don't do public affection. Or I can just—"

"No, I, uh..." I cleared my throat, straightening my back, and I did everything in my power to not blush. I didn't have enough power. I blushed. "So... I've been thinking about it, you know? Trying to... save my first kiss for somebody special. And I think it's eating me alive, because I feel like I have to choose right with the first person

I kiss, and so I'm never going to be with anyone in my *life* at this rate." I was talking too quickly. I did that when I was nervous. And I was really nervous right now. I should have thought this through, but if I did, then I would have backed out. "So I guess I just... want to get the first kiss done and over with. With somebody I trust. And... so... I was wondering if you could just... you know."

Her lips parted, and her eyebrows went high. I shifted anxiously from one foot to the other. Was it possible to die of embarrassed tension? No, probably not. Otherwise I'd be a charred skeleton by now.

"If you want to," I said, my throat tight. "I mean—I'm sure you didn't come to Castle Hollow looking for some clueless nobody to kiss. I was just figuring since it might come in handy at the dance tomorrow—"

"I certainly wouldn't *mind* it," she said, and my stomach flopped because maybe she was going to kiss me and I didn't know what to *expect* or think or feel or do or how to breathe or how to stand up straight or how to exist right now. Lyra furrowed her brow. "But... despite your little crisis of faith, I'd still want your first kiss to be special."

"I—um. If you don't want to, then you don't have to. Obviously."

"It's not that." A smile played across her lips. "So... you're asking me to give you your first kiss."

"Um..." My brain fizzled out. I could at least check this off the list. Gloria had told me to make more bad choices, and I'd done it in record time. "I... guess so. Would you mind? I know that's a little weird. No, actually, I think it's very weird. But..."

"After dinner." She leaned back against the counter, a smile playing over her features. "I don't like to disappoint a woman. I want you to get the proper first-kiss experience."

"The proper—um—what?" Now my heart was pounding so hard I could barely hear anything else.

"You seem like you're into cute romance," she said. "I'm sure you've fantasized of what a first kiss would look like. Out under the stars? In the backseat of a car far away from civilization?"

"Oh, wow. You're trying to fulfill my fantasies. Okay. Um. That's unexpected. Not bad, for the record. Unexpected in a very good way. Am I rambling? I think maybe I'm rambling. I'm not blushing too much, am I?"

Lyra smiled wider, reaching up and brushing back a loose strand of my hair. "You are about as red as the holly berries you love so much around the place. So, go on."

"Uh—" I squirmed. "I don't know. I think—comfy? At home, probably. I feel like I want it to be safe. I guess after a nice meal and a movie and just hanging out staying up late together looking at the stars through the window, and... then just... you know." I pressed my fingers together, the best I could do to illustrate a kiss because saying *and then kissing* would kill me on the spot.

She laughed softly. "That's so perfectly like you, Piper. So... what would you like for dinner tonight? Shall I take you out somewhere? Or I can cook for us."

"I—um." Was this what dating someone actually felt like? Or just what dating Lyra would be like? She had to just be special. She was amazing and had all the hallmarks of a perfect partner. I was so ridiculously jealous all of a sudden because *I* wanted to date Lyra. Why couldn't I have actually been a lesbian? Why couldn't the entire town of Castle Hollow have been right about my sexuality? "I think... whatever you like works well for me."

She looked me over and I kind of burned under her gaze. I wondered what she saw when she looked at me. Did she think I was pretty? Did she think about kissing me? She smiled, and this time it felt like I was winning a whole list of prizes. "Let's go out for dinner," she said. "And we can pick something up from the bakery and bring it back for dessert. And maybe then we can put on a fire, cuddle in blankets and watch a movie, watch the stars, and then if you're still feeling up to it, we can..." And with a quirk of an eyebrow and her lips pulled up into a smile, she pressed her fingers together, imitating my awkward symbol for *and then we kiss*. I ducked my head.

"You're, um—good at this."

"Thanks," she laughed. "My ex always complained I was crap at events and planning personal time. I'm trying to practice and improve a little. Plus, you're such a natural at getting people together for a good time, I think you're a good inspiration for me."

My face was hotter than the surface of the sun. On a hot day. Did the sun have hot days and colder days? I figured it probably didn't, but if it did, I'd be one of the hot days. "I want to say something good and clever in response, but, um, I've got nothing."

"That's fine too," she laughed, pushing past me. "I'll head up to the rental house."

"What—how come? Don't tell me *that's* where we're—"

"Absolutely not. But I have to get my stuff. I want to dress nicely if this is our first date."

The fuse blew in my brain. "Uh—dress. Yeah! For sure. I'm going to… wear something too. Well, I mean, yeah, probably a given. I'd probably get really cold otherwise. And can you imagine the looks?" I laughed nervously. "No. Not wearing something. I mean—not *just* wearing something. I'll wear something nice."

She smiled wider, stopping by the door with her travel mug in hand and glancing back at me. "I can't wait to see."

I had no idea how she just *said words* so easily. She lived in a whole other world I knew not of.

I fussed through my clothes for a while before I settled on a deep jade-green dress, layering on leggings and a jacket, but I still figured it out too quickly—I paced the floor in my living room so anxious I wanted to rip my hair out and scream as I waited for Lyra to get back, and by the time I finally heard a knock at my door, I jumped out of my skin getting it.

"Hey—oh." I stopped at the sight of my neighbor Sarah, a woman in her late forties with dark blonde hair and tired brown eyes, bundled up in about three separate jackets as she handed a box over to me. I tried not to look disappointed to see her. "Hi, Sarah."

"This is yours. Got misdelivered to my place." She paused. "Something wrong?"

"No! Just... um..." I tried to laugh normally. It sounded like a hyena on speed. "Just a nice... date tonight with my girlfriend. I thought it was her knocking. Sorry. Thanks so much! You're the best."

She softened into a smile. "I heard about that girlfriend. You know, I always—"

"Always thought I'd end up with a woman, right?"

She stopped, eyebrows raised. "I was saying, I always hoped you'd find someone to treat you right. You give so much to other people, and you deserve someone to give you that, too."

"Oh." I cleared my throat. "Thank you... that's really sweet of you."

She smiled wider. "But I *was* always pretty sure you'd end up with a woman."

Unbelievable. I forced a smile. "Well, you were right!"

"I've heard how you've come alive ever since you and Lyra got together. I can't wait to see the dance—and the whole festival. I think Castle Hollow is coming back."

I collapsed on my sofa with the box cast aside a second later, just breathing out slowly.

Seriously, *why* everyone had always thought I was a lesbian, I wasn't sure. I'd never really liked any of the boys, but they just weren't the best choices. I was *really* sad when Katie moved away, but that was just because we were friends. These were all normal things.

Of course, maybe getting this nervous over kissing my friend, when it was expressly just to get my first kiss done, wasn't the most normal straight girl thing.

When another knock came from the door, I jumped up and tripped over myself with a gasp, crashing into the door before I righted myself, smoothed out my dress, and put on a cool face before I opened it. What little bit of my composure I'd gotten back, though, I lost when I saw Lyra in a pantsuit with a tie, her hair tied up, looking like... um... well, nice. She looked nice. Really nice.

"Hi," I said, my voice just a breathy little thing. She gave me a concerned smile.

"Should I ask what the crashing and banging was?"

"Oh, uh, I tripped over my foot and collided face-first with the door."

She put a hand on her hip. "Should I be upset the door stole your first kiss before I could get it?"

The fuse blew in my brain again. "Um... I hope you weren't planning on kissing me like that. That would probably hurt us both."

She laughed, and her eyes sparkled. Was it gay to think about how a woman's eyes *sparkled* when she laughed? "I was planning on a bit more delicacy," she said. "But if you want to know the specifics, well... how about we go to dinner first?"

Wow. Yeah, whoever was going to get to date Lyra was seriously lucky. Was it gay to want to claw someone's face off for getting to date this woman when I wouldn't?

"Let's," I said. "Um... wait. I forgot to get a reservation or—"

"I took care of it," she laughed, reaching out for my hand. "You look beautiful tonight, Piper. Shall we?"

"We... shall." I took her hand, and I got a few heart-pounding steps down the path to her car before she cleared her throat.

"Do you want to lock your door?"

"I completely forgot I even had a house." I doubled back to lock the door before I followed her, this time, out to the car and slid into the passenger seat.

And as if I wasn't feeling enough weirdness already, she smiled at me as she started the car and turned on the local Christmas music station, and she backed out onto the street to the sound of *Silver Bells*.

"You're really picking up the Christmas spirit," I said, and she laughed.

"I've had a good source of inspiration."

We talked and laughed the whole way to the restaurant, but under the surface I was still in total panic mode navigating the thoughts about kissing. Was it normal to be this nervous? It was just because it was my first, right? That had to be all.

She took me to my absolute favorite, a Mexican place close to the town center, and when I gushed about how much I loved it she gave me a coy smile and said, "I know. I asked Gloria your favorite place."

"You asked Gloria?"

"I figured if anyone knew random information about someone and would be willing to share it at the drop of a hat..."

Well, she wasn't wrong. But the way the woman paid attention to me and did all these little things for that made my heart throb, I was getting really emotional. It tore me up into little bits even while we sat in the booth seat near the kitchen that had been my favorite spot here since I was eleven.

This felt like a whole component of life that was *really* special and really important, and I'd neglected it all along. And now that I was here, I wanted it for real—wanted someone who'd look at me like Lyra did, who'd take me out to places like this and laugh with me like Lyra did, who made me better like Lyra did.

"What are you getting?" she said, scanning her menu.

"Holiday tacos."

She looked up. "Holiday what?"

"They're *delicious*," I gushed. "It's like Thanksgiving dinner in a taco. Turkey, cranberry sauce, mashed potatoes…"

She wrinkled her nose. "I'm going to be honest, sweetheart, that sounds absolutely disgusting. But I support you getting it if it makes you happy."

"You should try them, too!"

"Thanks for the offer. I would die first."

The holiday tacos were delicious, because *of course* they were. You could never go wrong with holiday tacos. And Lyra made a face and leaned back in her seat when I offered them to her, but we both laughed about it all through the meal, and once we finished, pulling my jacket tighter and nestling against Lyra's side against the cold when we stepped out into the flurrying snow just felt natural. She was warm. And I liked her a lot.

Hitting up the bakery together, Colin behind the counter lit up at the sight of us both and mentioned how he'd *heard* about me and my girlfriend, and I got to make the introductions. Watching Lyra talk and laugh together with my old friend was a mushy mess inside my heart, and the ache just deepened as we got a tray of peppermint brownies and went back out to the car.

Letting Lyra go at the end of the month was going to suck. At least I'd be able to act out the pretend breakup well.

Going home alongside Lyra felt natural, and kicking off our boots while laughing over how I tried to take mine off while stealing a brownie at the same time, it was a little too comfortable and easy. When we put on the fire and curled up on the couch with brownies and *Miracle on 34th*

Street, which luckily her ex hadn't tainted, I rested my head on her shoulder, and she slipped an arm around my waist, and I thought I wanted to stay like this forever.

When our brownie plate only had crumbs left, our hot drinks ran out to just the dregs at the bottom, and Lyra turned off the TV and set the remote down, the sudden silence—just the fireplace crackling and the low wind against the windowpane—left me just with my racing thoughts and my pounding heart.

"Thanks for tonight," I said, my mouth as dry as if I'd stuffed the wool blanket in it. "It's been a lot of fun."

"I've had a lot of fun, too. Thanks for joining me." Her hand slipping up my back gave me chills, and when she craned her neck to look at me, I blushed and found I couldn't meet her gaze. "You know…"

"Y-yeah?" If she was backing out, I didn't know if it would be a disappointment or a relief.

But she went the exact opposite route. She took my chin between her thumb and forefinger, and my heart jumped when she turned my head to look at her. I struggled to breathe, my face hot, and she smiled wider.

"You really are beyond beautiful, Piper."

"Wh—what's beyond beautiful? Does it loop back around into ugly or something?"

She laughed softly, her thumb caressing the line of my jaw. I think I might have passed out. That would have been a mood kill. "It definitely doesn't. Just off into some magical territory where I can't believe *anyone* might be lucky enough to kiss you, let alone…"

I swallowed. "Um… I'm just like a *little* bit nervous right now, just so you know."

"Oh, just a little bit."

"Maybe more than a little bit."

Her expression turned more serious. "You know, we don't have to do this if you don't—"

"I do." It took me by surprise more than it did her, and it already took her by surprise. I swallowed, and I said it again, more softly this time. "I… do want to. If that's okay."

She stared down at my lips for a second before she whispered, reverently, like she was in a trance, "More than okay." She swiped her thumb gently over my lips, sending a thrill down my spine, and she leaned in closer. I think my hands shook. I couldn't really feel them. The fireplace smelled sweet, like toasted marshmallows, but Lyra smelled sweeter—like ginger and clove and woodsy like cedar, too, like warm things I just wanted to wrap myself up in. She whispered soft little words that made my head spin wild. "I'm going to kiss you now."

"P-please. I'm—" I cleared my throat. "I'm sorry if I suck at it or don't know what I'm doing."

Her smiled widened. "Don't worry. You can give it as many tries as you like. I'm sure you'll pick it up."

"You say that, but I'm an expert at missing things."

"You always remember the important things."

"I forgot I had a house just earlier."

She laughed softly. "Can I kiss you, or what?"

"I—yes, please."

She leaned in, and I closed my eyes and tried not to let my heart burst out of my chest, and when her lips brushed mine, I gasped, softly. She paused, not pulling away, but when I softened into the tenderness of her lips against mine, she sank into the kiss, and I was the most panicked and the most at-peace person in the history of the world.

So, this was what kissing felt like. This was what kissing *Lyra* felt like. A voice screamed in my head not to screw this up, that I'd remember this forever, but for once, my sense won and I let go without trying to be a million different things.

All I needed to be right now was the person Lyra was kissing. And she kissed me so well.

Her lips felt fuller than I'd expected against mine, soft and firm at the same time, silky as velvet but strong enough to capture my lips in hers and flood me with the feeling of her, the scent of her filling my senses. Electric pulses surged through my head, and I gripped tight at her waist and kissed her back, moving my lips slowly, the sounds of the kiss and the sounds of our breaths coming short suddenly the only sound in the world.

I'd always, always, always always always been oscillating between dreaming my first kiss would be magical and perfect and fearing I'd screw it up and it would just be a disappointment. I'd never imagined it would be this—that it would be so perfect and make my whole life feel like it was exploding at the same time.

Gloria was right, though. I wasn't going to do things right. I was just going to enjoy the moment, screw things up, and deal with the consequences later.

I really, really liked kissing Lyra.

Chapter 10

LYRA

Ah, dammit. This was a problem.

I'd already been nursing a crush on her over these past two weeks. I'd figured there was no harm—that she was just a cute straight girl who I might play-flirt with at most and then leave after a month—but then she banged into the kitchen and told me to kiss her.

My fault, really. Should have just pecked her on the lips and called it a day. Me with the self-indulgence again, and I ended up here like this, tangled up on the couch with her, caught up in the heat of a kiss touched with the taste of her tea and peppermint brownie, and I was *really* in too deep with this girl.

She gripped me tightly as we kissed, her shaking lips moving against mine in slow kisses, and gradually, her nervous breaths turned into small moans and gasps that built up in a longing ache between my thighs.

She'd asked me to take her first kiss, not her virginity. Still, my body didn't get the memo, especially not when she gripped handfuls of my shirt and let out those tiny, obscene moans against my lips.

I pulled back just an inch, parted my lips to ask her if it was okay, if she wanted to stop, but she chased my lips and caught me in another kiss. I grunted in surprise, and when I tipped backwards on the couch, she followed me until this *heterosexual woman* was honest-to-God pinning me down on the sofa beneath her, pressing her breasts against mine while we kissed. And Christ, it was aching between my legs.

I'd be damned if I wasn't going to enjoy the moment, though. I trailed my hands up and down her back, feeling her gentle musculature through the soft fabric of her dress, and when I nipped lightly at her bottom lip, Piper straight-up *moaned* against my mouth and ground her hips against mine. A spike of arousal shot through me, and I tugged away from the kiss.

"Piper—"

"Sorry." She pushed herself up, eyes wide, but Piper propped up on her hands just above my face wasn't really less of a turn-on. "Is this not good?"

"No, it's… it's good." I shifted underneath her, propping up onto one arm. "Is this what you want?"

She just stared wordlessly, wide-eyed, for a second before she nodded. "Is that okay?"

God, I was giving this woman a sexual awakening. If I had any sense, I'd back out now. But how was I supposed to have sense seeing her on top of me like this? "More than okay," I said, feeling my voice get deep and thick, and I pressed my lips to hers again. She moaned into the kiss like she couldn't have waited a second longer, and she sank down with me, pinning me against the couch cushion and kissing me.

I gripped her by the hips and touched my tongue to her lips, and she gasped, and when she parted her lips and granted me entry, she ground her hips against me again. It sent a wild flush of arousal through me, and I met her this time, gripping her hips tighter and moving mine with her. She let out an obscene groan into my mouth, but I didn't stop, and neither did she. Her tongue met mine in desperate, clumsy motions, swirling around mine, and it built up the desperate need aching in my core.

If I took this woman tonight, I was going to regret it like hell. But somehow I couldn't get my mind around that one right now.

She parted breathless and red-faced, hovering just over my face with a hooded gaze, and she breathed, "Is it always like this...?"

"Not always," I said, gliding my hands up and down her sides. "Sometimes it's boring. Sometimes it's gross. And sometimes it's mind-blowing."

A smile ghosted over her lips. "This is definitely more of the mind-blowing kind."

Oh, I could blow her mind. I wanted her in the armchair, legs spread wide, while I knelt in front of her. I bit my lip. "I'm definitely enjoying this too."

"I'm not too—you know—clumsy, awkward?"

I snorted. "Hardly. God, you're sexy." It was only after the words left my mouth that I realized they'd gone too far—given a name to the elephant in the room—but she didn't shy away. She reddened, but she bit her lip and, holding eye contact with me, thrust her hips against me again.

Jesus. Was Piper trying to *top* me right now?

I lifted my hips to meet her, gasping softly at the sensation. She didn't give me a chance to catch up—she moved her hips against mine again, shifting slightly to put more of her weight on my core, and I lost it. I spread my legs tighter, slipped my hands down and gripped her ass, and I pressed her firmer into me. She groaned at the sensation, and then boldly, firmly, she ducked back in and pressed another kiss to my lips. Somehow her tongue found its way into my mouth, and I surrendered to the sensation of her tongue exploring, swirling around mine.

I was sure she'd be able to tell soon, even through the pants, what kind of effect she was having on me. But I wasn't the only one—her dress rode up, and I felt how much heat was building between her thighs.

I wanted her viscerally and primally, in a raw and crude way stripped of all our decencies. Something about her awakened a hungry need in me, and I was powerless against it.

I moved my hands down to her leggings under her dress, hiking her dress up, and then like she hadn't surprised me enough yet, Piper pitched up and reached back, tugging her leggings down her ass with one quick, callous move. I wasn't asking any questions. I hooked my thumbs under the band of her leggings, just below the hem of her simple pink underwear, and I pulled them down to her knees. She moved with me, shifting her legs and letting me work them down the rest of the way, and I dropped the leggings on the floor, moving my hands back up and hiking her dress up until I could feel the wetness on her underwear against my pants.

She pressed deeper into the kiss and undid the top button of my shirt, and I reached back and undid the next before she caught my wrist, lifting up from the kiss and looking at me with hunger in her eyes.

"I want to do it," she said, her voice husky as she moved her hand down to the next button.

I wasn't complaining. Hell of a way to mark her first kiss.

She rose to straddle me, and she undid the rest of my shirt buttons. Somehow, I found myself flushing and nervous under her attention as she slid my shirt off, tossing it to the floor, and looking over my body from where she straddled my waist. She let out a soft sigh, tracing a hand over my stomach.

"You are so pretty," she whispered.

"Want to tell me what's on the table right now?" I said, my voice shaky and a little less cool than I thought it would be. She laughed, softly, ducking her head as she blushed.

"Um... am I going too far?"

"I'll stop you if you do anything too much."

She bit her lip. "I just..." But she gave up on whatever it was she was saying, fussing with the button on my pants instead. I reached to undo them, but she tightened her grip and did it herself, popping open the button before, slowly—reverently—pulling down the zipper, one tooth at a time.

Dammit, but it turned out she was good at this. I think I was soaked already.

She slid my pants down, settling between my legs and looking like a sexy goddess with her red curls all in every direction, my pants in her hand. She held them up, and then—I swear to god this woman—she *folded them*, just quickly, and laid them on the table. I reached up, put my hands on her hips, but she rose a little, took the fabric of her dress in her hands, and pulled it over her head—and then that too, folded and set down.

"I'd like to kiss you again now," she said, settling on top of me again, and I was powerless to do much other than hand myself over to this woman.

I kissed her, my hands exploring the soft skin of her back, and when our kiss deepened to tugging on lips and touching tongues, she pressed her center against mine and thrust, once. I jerked my back up off the couch, moving with her, and she broke from the kiss and threw her head back, letting out the sexiest moan I'd heard in my life. My hands fell to her bra clasp.

"Can I take this off?" I wasn't in control of what I was saying or doing anymore. She nodded, breathlessly, and I worked her bra off in one swift, clean motion, pulling it down her arms and dropping it on top of her dress. I slid my hands to her breasts, brushing my thumbs over her nipples—hard as diamonds for me already—and she groaned and sat up, putting her hands on mine and cupping them against her breasts. She shifted between my legs, putting more of her weight on where her core met mine, and it drove me wild, needing our underwear gone.

I couldn't last much longer. I sat up and kissed her again as I hooked my fingers under the band of her underwear, and she responded immediately, moving to let me slide them down and over her ankles, dropping them on the floor. She caught the band of my sports bra before I could do anything, and I shimmied out of it as she lifted it up—and then as if she hadn't blown me out of the water enough already, she bent down and took my nipple in her mouth before I could even say a word.

Dammit, this woman was going to break me. I threw my head back and let out a long, shaky curse, gripping her by the back of the head and holding her against me, and when she slipped a hand down my front and teased under the band of my underwear, I collapsed, suddenly shaky in every part of me. She moved with me, coming down on top of me and tugging my underwear down just a little, meeting my eyes with a heady, heavy look in hers.

"Can I take these off?" she said, as if there was a world in which I'd say no.

"Of course. Just—are you—sure you want this?"

She nodded. "I want to try making you feel good. Um... I assume you like doing this kind of thing. I just hope I'm okay at it."

"I can tell you already you're going to do great," I groaned, collapsing back on the couch as she slipped my underwear off and laid it on top of the rest of my clothes. She let out a small, soft breath looking at where I was *probably* getting her couch wet, but I couldn't really care right now.

"Oh, Lyra," she whispered. "You're beautiful."

I squirmed a little, uncharacteristically shy. I was more used to quick passionate sessions, getting right to it, not the soft reverence, the whispered compliments about how good I looked.

Leave it to Piper to turn everything I was used to upside-down. "I'm... glad you like what you see."

"I love it." She paused. "Um... Lyra... what do I do?"

"I'm guessing you have one yourself, so, uh... I think you can figure it out."

She looked down, blushing, but she didn't say anything—just trailed her fingers slowly up my thigh, up until the touch of her against my center absolutely tore my world in half. I groaned, clutching at the sofa cover, and I watched as she trailed her fingers slowly through my folds, teasing over my clit. When she applied a little more pressure, moved a little quicker against me, I felt the edges of my consciousness melt away until everything felt like a hazy dream.

A really amazing wet dream.

"Tell me what feels good, okay?" she said, gently, her voice as sweet as if her fingers weren't playing with my clit. "And what doesn't. I can take feedback."

I propped myself up on one elbow. "You can take feedback, huh?"

She smiled. "Of course. Always on the quest for improvement, you know?"

This woman had never even *kissed* someone before, and frankly? I was getting the idea she was going to be better at sex than anyone I'd been with before. Suddenly I was *intensely* jealous at who was going to get to have her.

Hell, what was I thinking? She clearly wasn't straight. Maybe *I* could have her. I wanted her, and badly at that. Especially if we could make this happen again. There was no point thinking about this. I just wanted to feel her against me and lose myself in how damn good it felt when she touched me, when she *looked* at me like she did.

"Then—inside me, please," I said, and she let out a sharp breath before she bit her lip, nodding.

"Just let me know what feels good." She slid a finger down to my entrance, and slowly, exploring, slipped it inside me. Feeling the way she filled me up, even just with one slender finger inching deeper inside me until I felt her knuckle against me, I lost it, moaning obscenely and moving my hip to match her—to get more of her. She bit her lip harder. "Good?"

"So good." I shifted. "Can you... bend your finger a little more?"

I felt her finger crook against where I was most sensitive, flooding me with that electric sensation. "Like this?"

"God, Piper, you're perfect," I groaned, collapsing back against the couch. "Please don't stop."

She was a natural, turned out. She slid her finger out and thrust back in, and I felt an orgasm starting to build before long. At my desperate request, she added a second finger, shifting her position to pump harder in and out of me, and I spread my legs wider and gave myself over to her. I shouted her name over and over in between curses, thrusting my hips against her, and she kept going until I crashed over the edge into the sweet oblivion of orgasm, pulsating hard on her fingers and arching my back higher and higher on the couch.

I collapsed hard, hot and sweaty and breathing hard, and she met me with no hesitation, kissing me fiercely. I gripped her tightly and kissed her back as hard as I could, tongues swirling in a hot, wet, obscene dance before she propped herself up above me.

"Um... did you like that?" she said, eyes gleaming with a light that said she knew damn well I liked that.

"You think I would come like that if I didn't?"

She laughed nervously, biting her lip. "Um... maybe I was just hoping for a compliment."

I pressed myself up and captured her in a fierce kiss before I pulled away breathless. "You are a goddess, you feel unbelievably good, you have *no* idea how beautiful you are—"

"Oh, please," she laughed nervously, ducking her head. "I wasn't ready for *this* many compliments—"

"And I think it's cute that you fold everything."

"Oh! I—um—" She looked over at the folded clothes. "If we're being honest, I didn't even think about that. It just felt right. Um... that's embarrassing."

I was definitely in too deep with this girl. I pressed a kiss against her lips, and she murmured softly against me, kissing me back. When I pulled away, I spoke in a deep, husky voice. "I want to take you."

"Take me? Um... what do you mean? Take me where?"

I paused. "Really?"

She blushed harder. "Um... I'm sorry. What?"

I laughed, shaking my head. "You sweet, precious little thing, Piper. I want to touch you. I want to pleasure you. I want to make you come."

"Oh—you—" She went wide-eyed. "Do you want to do that?"

"More than you know. You are so sexy, and I just want to make you feel good." I paused. "If... that's okay."

She pursed her lips, wide-eyed, but she nodded. "Um... if there's anything in particular you like..."

"Please. Try telling me what you like? You should let someone else do something for you for once."

She laughed nervously. "Okay. Point taken. But, um... it's... you know, it's my first time, so... it's not like I know a lot about what I like or don't."

"Great. Then I'll just start gentle and you can tell me what you like and what you don't like."

She blushed harder, but she nodded. "That, uh—that sounds great! I'm better at receiving feedback than giving it, just so you know. I'm a bit awkward."

"You can let me know anything. I want you to feel good."

She was achingly beautiful sprawled out underneath me on the couch. She didn't need to worry about any problems with giving feedback— her body responded loud and clear to everything I did, nearly lifting herself up off the sofa when I touched her. She moaned loud and cried my name as I worked my fingers over her clit, gripped tight at my wrist and gasped half-words as I thrust my fingers into her, and when I couldn't help myself any longer and I buried my face between her legs, she nearly screamed my name before she came, throbbing hard on my mouth, crying out so loud it lit me up until I thought I'd come just hearing it.

Oh, we definitely weren't done tonight. We were going to learn an awful lot about what the other liked tonight.

Chapter 11

PIPER

I woke up in nothing but my panties next to a naked woman, and I think I panicked for a solid ten seconds lying there listening to her breathe.

It hadn't really sunk in what I was doing last night. It had just been one thing leading to another. I'd wanted to have my first kiss in a safe place. And the next thing I knew, she was coming on my mouth.

She'd... tasted kind of nice. It had been hot. Was it gay to get turned on licking another woman's—

Okay, I didn't need to ask. That was definitely gay.

I didn't have long to pull myself together. We generally woke up around the same time—I knew that one full well from all the times we'd shared a bed now. Was it also gay I wanted to share a bed with her all the time?

Oh my god. What if I'd *always* been gay? Maybe I'd just never been interested in dating because there *were* no gay girls in my town when I was growing up. I'd always thought dating was just a low priority for me. But when I sat here and thought about it, I desperately wanted to be Lyra's girlfriend.

I was a raging lesbian. I couldn't *believe* I was the last person in town to figure it out.

I sat up in bed, moving quietly as the first traces of sunlight still made their way slowly into the room, casting Lyra in a beautiful golden light, but she still stirred at the movement. I froze, and when she stretched her arm and bumped my hip, she jolted, waking up with a start and freezing at the sight of me. I think she had the same *oh-crap-we're-naked* realization I did after waking up—she glanced down over my mostly-naked body and back up to me, eyes wide.

"Good... morning," she said, pushing herself slowly up to a seat. She looked down at herself, the blanket falling off her to reveal... um... yeah, I was gay. I tried not to stare. She glanced back at me, and I realized I was staring.

"H-hi. Good morning. Um... how are you doing? Did you sleep well?"

She looked away, rubbing her arm. "Sleep? Er... yeah. Slept... soundly."

"Okay, great. I'm glad. Me too. I think it's because I was exhausted when I went to sleep. I guess we... um." *Wore ourselves out going at it like rabbits?* I wasn't finishing that sentence.

Oh my god, this was the most awkward thing in my life. Way to get my first kiss, my first time having sex, my sexuality crisis, and then the most awkward thing in my life done all at once.

"Yeah, I... well, I always sleep soundly after—" She cut herself off, equally incapable of finishing sentences.

"Oh. Well. I, um... I hope that's good."

She sighed, rubbing her forehead, turning back to me. "Okay, I can't take it. Piper, we fucked like animals."

"I mean... what else were we going to fuck like, plants?" I wrung my hands. "Okay. Bad joke. Sorry. I get like that when I'm nervous. I'm a little nervous."

"A little nervous? You look like you're about to faint."

"I might be, like... medium nervous."

She sighed again, harder this time, and swung her legs off the bed to sit next to me. It took all my willpower to not stare at her body. I didn't use all my willpower—I stared at her body. The swell of her breasts, the curve of her waist and her hips... I'd never noticed anything like that on a person before. "So... I guess we should address the elephant in the room. That was the least straight thing I've ever seen from a straight girl, and I saw two of my straight-girl friends dance topless to Lady Gaga once."

"Which song?"

"That's not what's important right now. Are you *sure* you're straight?"

I cleared my throat. "Um... so... define straight."

"Exclusively attracted romantically and sexually to men."

"Oh. That's a thorny definition." I scratched my neck. "Um... I think I might be a little bit gay."

"That's what I was afraid of," she sighed, rubbing her forehead. I winced.

"Um... I'm sorry. Is that bad?"

"No, it's not bad." She sighed again, each time a little more desperate than the last until she sounded this time like she was just wishing for Santa's elves to come in the room and whisk her away. "The problem is that I think you're cute and very attractive, and I was counting on you being straight to make sure that never turned into anything serious."

I blinked fast. "*You* think *I'm* attractive?"

She gave me a wry smile. "You seem to think I'm some kind of Aphrodite and you're just a lowly nothing. You really have no idea how gorgeous you are, do you?"

"Well, just—" I flushed. "I'm nothing special. I'm just a weird girl who loves Christmas and lives in some town where nothing ever happens—"

"You are a beautiful young woman who *makes* things happen, and it turns out I find that very attractive, so—yes, Piper, I'm very attracted to you. And I'm not looking to rebound immediately from my breakup with someone who's married to this town I'm definitely not interested in living in."

And there was the rub. First kiss, first time having sex, first time handing my heart to somebody, and first time having it broken, all in rapid-fire succession. I looked down. "I get that. Um... thank you. Even if we can't be anything more than this, I... you know... it means a lot that you like me like that too. That you think I'm attractive."

She arched an eyebrow at me. "Too?"

"I definitely like you." I kicked under the bed. "Even as a fake girlfriend, dating you has been really nice. If I were to imagine a world where we could keep doing that for real, um... I think I'd like that world quite a lot."

She sank back on the bed, staring out the windows at the Christmas light cutting a soft glow against the early dawn sky. I slid to my feet.

"But, as the head of the cultural committee, I'm still here to make your stay enjoyable. So... some coffee?"

"You did an excellent job last night of making my stay enjoyable, I'll tell you that."

I paused. "That makes it sound like the cultural committee has a prostitution ring. I think we might get into trouble with state government if we did that."

"Let's go out for coffee. I want you to get your peppermint mocha."

She could have prefaced anything with *let's go out* and made me want to do it. I hunched my shoulders and nodded, looking away. "That sounds really nice. Maybe we can get some croissants while we're out. Right now?"

"You might want to put clothes on."

"Oh... I kind of forgot about that." I covered up my breasts, heat building in my face. She sighed, a smile spreading over her face.

"So, runs in the family."

"Look—shush."

She laughed, and I could have lived forever on that sound. I was still only getting a month of it, though, no matter how much cultural committee work I was putting in to make her like it here.

It hung heavy on my mind, even as we got dressed and went out talking and laughing like everything was normal on our way to the bakery, and it got to be a little too much by the time we were back at my kitchen table, cradling our drinks in our hands between bites of almond croissant, *Have Yourself a Merry Little Christmas* playing from my phone speaker.

"So... what now?" I said quietly, the smell of peppermint and toasted pastry warm in the air but not quite enough to distract me from how messy my thoughts were right now. "Do we just pretend yesterday didn't happen? Do we just... keep on pretending we're girlfriends, even knowing how I feel?"

Lyra chewed her lip, looking out the window at the snow blanketing the ground, crisp white and pale blue in the morning light. "I'm... thinking about it. I know we have the dance tonight, for one thing."

"Well, yeah. We do."

"And you're right, that it's a couples' event. Probably best if we kiss."

I dropped a piece of croissant, my face suddenly fiery-hot. "Um—yep."

She raised her eyebrows. "You okay?"

"I'm... good. Great." Just thinking about her kissing me. And how my heart was probably going to react if she kissed me in front of *everyone* in town.

"If you'd rather we didn't—"

"No, I wouldn't rather we didn't. I would rather we did. What? Hold on, let me figure out sentences." I shook my head. "I want to kiss you. I mean, at the dance! Not just in general. I mean, I do want to kiss you just in general, but not at the dance. I mean—no—wait—back up—"

She reached across the table and put a hand down on mine. "Take your time," she said, a smile playing on her lips.

"I—do want that. Just... you *know*."

"I don't know."

I gave her a vague, frustrated gesture. "You *know*. What if I... um... like..."

"I'm going to need more information."

I put a hand over my mouth, looking away as I mumbled. "It's going to turn me on a lot."

She laughed. I fumed.

"Don't laugh! This is serious! I... like you, you know."

"I'm laughing because it's nothing to be worried about." She leaned back in her chair. "If you want to repeat last night, I'm down. Just because I'm not ready for a relationship doesn't mean I don't want to do these things."

I paused. "Um... are you... talking about some kind of casual fling?"

"Why not? You can explore your sexuality and figure things out. I'll definitely enjoy it. Things don't have to be forever to be good in the now."

I paused, staring at her for the longest time until she shifted awkwardly.

"Did I say something weird?"

"No, just... not a way I'd really thought about things before." I looked down into the towering whipped cream of my mocha, dotted with peppermint candy. "So... that's something you think you'd like."

"Only if it's something you think you'd like. I want to be very clear with what I want, and present it with no pressure for you to respond one way or the other."

I cradled my coffee, breathing in the sweet, chocolatey scent of it. "Well," I said, finally, "I guess... if we're going to be around one another all the time anyway while you're still in Castle Hollow... it's not like..."

"Again, you don't have to."

Maybe this was a good thing, actually. If Lyra were staying—if this could have turned into some kind of long-term thing—then I'd have crushed myself to death with pressure to *do it right.*

Come to think of it, Lyra was probably giving me the best opportunity I could have ever had. Zero pressure, just getting to explore my feelings—and kiss her too.

It was probably going to hurt at the end of December, but I guess sometimes things that might hurt could still be worth it.

"Can I kiss you right now, then?" I said, and she blinked, eyebrows going high.

"That's quite the direct response."

I laughed, scratching the back of my head. "Well... I don't see any reason to beat around the bush when I know what I want. You're really pretty, you know. It's kind of wild."

She stood up, walking over to my side of the table, and she put a finger under my chin again, just like last night—tilting me up to look at her. Something dropped in the pit of my stomach, and I felt my whole body react, lighting up aching for her.

"You know what else is wild?" she said.

"Ostriches?"

She paused. "Those are definitely wild too. But I was thinking about how you are absolutely beautiful as well."

"Oh—that is pretty hard to wrap my head around, honestly—"

She bent down and pressed a kiss to my lips. I grunted against her lips, but the feeling of her against me was like plugging in the Christmas lights and seeing everything come alive, seeing everything come together, and I was surprised I didn't faint on the spot. I threw my arms around her neck and I kissed her back, and I just tried to tell myself to enjoy the moment and not think about the end of the month.

Chapter 12

LYRA

No doubt about it, the dance was pure Christmas magic. The maintenance people had been in and out under my and Piper's occasional supervision through the past week, and the run-down, sorry state of things in the community center was patched up—at least in the main hall.

It had been a bit of a rush getting here to coordinate with the decorations team—I'd kissed Piper over breakfast, and I swear I'd been planning on just a safe, chaste kiss until she stood with me, hooked her leg around me, and moaned while she ground her hips against me. Suddenly *chaste* was the last thing on my mind.

A happy couple of orgasms later, we went scrambling out the door still pulling our things together, laughing breathlessly as we did, but we still made it two minutes before the team arrived—just enough time to pull it together and not look like we'd almost missed the team by getting frisky. As much as I'd already liked her, I was really liking the wild flush and sparkle in her eyes Piper got when she played fast and loose with things.

I took charge directing the team—half scrabbled-together hands from town and half hired help from out of town—as we organized dressing the community center hall for a dance, setting up decorations over every inch of the place until it sparkled like Santa's workshop full of lights. Piper took on the just-as-critical task of managing morale, distributing cookies and hot drinks to our staff, chatting about Christmas magic, and we stepped in a few times to help out too—wrapping the tree in ribbon together, a few people standing close laughing and making comments at the way Piper giggled when our fingers touched exchanging the ribbon between our hands.

I was shameless, I admit, sneaking in little kisses between tasks. But Piper, for once, let herself be just as self-indulgent too, and we finished the decorations with an hour to spare anyway. Piper gave half the team crushing hugs all in turn, thanking them all for their contributions and gushing about how happy she was to see Christmas in Castle Hollow come back.

And once it was just the two of us waiting down the minutes until the event started, she laughed, twirling through the center of the room, her swishy dress flicking around her hips, softly lit by the glow of the Christmas lights all around. She beamed at me mid-twirl, and then it turned to panic as she lost her balance, nearly collapsing into a bough of tinsel. I caught her by the waist, and she giggled, leaning against me.

"My savior," she said.

"Someone's got to keep you from knocking over everything in this place."

She pecked my lips quickly, eyes shining. "I appreciate you. And so do the decorations. You know, I wouldn't have been able to put together an event like this without your help. If it works out—and I just *know* it will—it's all thanks to you."

"Hardly. I just handled logistics." I put my hands on her hips. "You're the only one with enough infectious enthusiasm to make something like this work."

"Oh, stop, you're flattering me." She laughed. "So... since we have a minute before everyone arrives... do you think we should practice our dance?"

"Do you know how to dance?"

She laughed. "Not a clue! But you look competent."

"A bold assertion, but here we go."

We put on the music—a cover of *Silent Night* by country music singer Brooke Carston—and we took off dancing slowly to the soothing melody, our shoes clicking on the hardwood floor.

When we finished, Piper looked at me like I'd hung the moon, and I wasn't quite sure how to handle someone looking at me that way—someone who, it turned out, was very gay, very available, and very interested—and she fell into me, pressing her lips to mine in a soft, sweet kiss that felt like coming home even though I wasn't sure what I'd been trying to come home to.

I wasn't thinking about things too much right now, though. I held her, and I kissed her, and it felt perfect, until a voice interrupted us from behind, and of everyone, it had to be Piper's mom saying, "Oh! You're making out. I can leave you to it."

Piper fell backwards away from me, whirling on where Louisa Fairway stood on the other side of the Christmas tree, wearing a long swishy pale gold dress. Piper was white as snow as she said, "Mom!? Oh my god. Where did you come from?"

Louisa beamed. "Outside. Oh! But before that, home. Hi, sweetie. Where is everyone?"

Piper shook her head. "Mom, it starts at four."

"Isn't it four now?" She fussed with her clutch until she got her phone out, and she laughed. "Oh! I must have forgotten to set the clocks back."

"Oh my god, Mom, it's December. And how did you get inside? Did you go through the back?"

"The parking spaces were clearer in the back."

Piper rubbed her forehead. "You're not supposed to go through the back rooms, Mom. That's why the no entry sign was there."

Louisa put a finger to her chin. "Oh... it was closer to the window, so I thought it was saying to go in through the door, not through the window."

"Mom, everyone knows you're not supposed to go through the window." Piper was rubbing her temples now. I smiled at Louisa.

"Hi, Mrs. Fairway. It's nice to see you here."

Louisa waved me off. "Oh, please. You can just call me Louisa. Or Mom. Why not just cut to the chase?"

I forced a polite smile. "That's very sweet of you to offer, Louisa, but I think I'll stick with that for now."

A *bump* sounded from the back, and Piper stiffened. "Mom, do you know what that sound is?"

Louisa just shrugged. "Probably your father. He saw something interesting in the back and went to go look at it."

"Oh my god." Piper started off towards the back, breaking out into a half-run as another *bump* came from the backroom. Louisa turned to me with a smile, and I forced my smile to stay natural.

"Olive couldn't make it?"

"Olive?" A look of surprise flashed over her face. "Oh! I forgot she could make it. Yes, she was in the car. I bet she fell asleep in the back. She sleeps a lot. She'll come in when she wakes up."

I sighed. "How about we go find her now? I don't want her to get cold."

"Oh, don't worry. I left the car running. The keys are in the ignition."

I paused. "You... left the keys in the ignition."

"Of course. I'd just lose my keys somewhere if I brought them with me. Can you imagine?" She laughed.

I didn't know how this woman had survived to nearly fifty. I forced my smile wider. "Well... how about we have Piper look after your keys? She's trustworthy."

"Oh! That's so smart. Piper picked a good one," she laughed. "You know, I'm really glad Piper found someone like you. She needed someone to look after her, remind her she deserves good things too. I worry about her working herself to the bone all the time."

"Yeah…" I looked up towards the back, where I could hear Piper's voice along with more clattering. The poor girl. Maybe I *did* need to stay longer in Castle Hollow, if just to keep her from getting a head injury keeping her family alive.

Of course, at the rate my feelings were taking off without me, I'd find any excuse to stay in Castle Hollow.

"She's come a long way already," I said, looking back to Louisa. "Once that girl sets her sights on something, she doesn't let up on it. And apparently that includes growing as a person and standing up for herself more."

She laughed, waving me off. "Oh, she was done growing when she hit fifteen, little thing that she is."

There wasn't much sense in trying to hold a very deep conversation with Louisa Fairway. I smiled and nodded. "Let's go make sure your daughter's still alive in the car."

"Piper's in the car?"

"Other daughter, Louisa."

"Oh, yes! Olive's such a good kid. I'm so proud of her. She's studying for medical school, and she almost passed one of her classes this semester!"

Well, weren't we shooting high?

I went with Louisa out to the car, and she didn't seem that panicked when it turned out Olive wasn't in the car—which was, indeed, left with the engine running and everything—but we followed the footprints in the snow from the backseat down to a coffee shop, where we found Olive walking away from the counter with an iced coffee the size of her head. She didn't seem to notice us, even when Louisa pointed to her and said, "See, there she is. All fine."

I sighed. "All fine. I do wonder how they both survived to adulthood..."

Louisa cocked her head. "What do you mean?"

"Nothing. Let's head back to the community center."

She had her hands shoved in her coat pocket as we walked back out into the fading light of the late afternoon, heading up towards the community center. "You know," she said, quietly, after walking quietly halfway there, "sometimes I've thought Piper should leave this town."

I glanced over at her. "How come?"

"Well, look at it." She gestured around at the shuttered shopfronts, the empty streets. "There's nothing happening here. There's nobody her age. Everyone's leaving. And poor Piper's pouring everything about herself into this town and getting nothing out of it. I just want her to be happy. It's what every mom wants. Except for terrible moms, but I don't think I'm a terrible mom."

Well, she did forget her child in the car and go to a party. But I wasn't saying that out loud. "Piper loves this place, though," I said, and she sighed.

"She really does. But it's a very uneven love. You know when you see the couples in the old movies where the wife does so many things for the husband but she doesn't get anything out of it? Lucky dear sweet Charlie isn't like that, because I can't do anything right, but neither can he, so we're both just trying our best to get anything done, but we have fun. What was I saying?"

"Piper and Castle Hollow."

"What about them?" She cocked her head. "Oh! Yes. It's like that. Piper loves the place and does so many things for it. Gives so much of herself for it. But I think she doesn't know how to expect anything in return. I just wish she could have lived in the place I did—the Castle Hollow that was so full of life, young and old, bankers and musicians, Black and white. Where the streets were full of people and you'd walk to the toy shop for a Christmas gift and say hi to all your friends along the way... she might be living in the same place geographically, but that old Castle Hollow is gone. Now it's just a bunch of us old middle-class white people who don't leave our houses unless we have to."

I wondered if she was secretly insightful deep down, or if this was just the equivalent of a stoner saying what they thought was really deep in between bong hits.

Still, I had to admit, Piper and her mom had a few things in common. Wild red hair, an absentminded streak, and a deep love for the town of old where people felt connected. And when I thought about it, Castle Hollow as they described it sounded a whole lot more interesting than Michael Landgrave's vision of six-lane streets between million-dollar prefab houses all lined up like toy soldiers for a company park.

Sometimes I'd felt like Piper seemed so much more *alive* than anyone else I knew. I'd always just chalked it up to her big, bright personality—the same one that got her conned into doing whatever anyone around her wanted her to. But maybe there was just something there about *caring* about something so damn much that life stood out as something more than just one day after another to work, come home, and sleep.

"I see what you mean," I said, and Louisa cocked her head.

"What I mean? What'd I say? I don't know if I really remember. I was zoning out a little."

Of course she was. I smiled. "Just that you think the dance is going to be fun."

"Oh! Yes, definitely. I can't wait."

I did see what she meant—that maybe Piper was giving all of herself for a town that didn't give her anything back.

But maybe the answer wasn't for Piper to stop giving to the town. Maybe it was for the town to start giving back to Piper.

We found Piper dragging her dad out of the back once we'd gotten back to the community center, Charles laughing the whole time and Piper looking less amused. Still, with Louisa and Charles distracted with one another, Piper came back over to me and clung to my side, holding my hand and looking at me with those big, warm brown eyes, and I found myself thinking a lot of things I shouldn't have been.

"Everything okay with my mom?"

"Yeah, just making sure your sister is alive. Apparently she snuck off to Baron's."

She laughed. "That's just like her. The girl has a caffeine addiction worse than her nap addiction."

"Well, I hear she's studying for med school. Caffeine goes with the program, right?"

Piper just sighed, a thousand-yard stare in her eyes. "*Studying* is a strong word..."

I took her hands. "Let's practice the dance one more time? We'll run the overhead sound system and make sure it holds up while we do."

"I would love to."

We danced, and no matter what music was playing, I found I couldn't take my eyes off Piper's. And even when the rest of the guests showed up, I couldn't look away from Piper.

We went from one place to another greeting guests, always together, my hand on her back and hers on mine as we talked to her oldest and dearest friends. Some came in from out of town, and she stumbled a little as she introduced me to all of them as her girlfriend, but self-indulgently as always, I just enjoyed it.

People surprised us by bringing gifts, an impromptu gift exchange a hundred ways between old friends, people who hadn't seen each other in years, and neighbors' friends' dog watchers' cousins. A dozen different gifts for Piper, and she gushed over each of them like they were the best things to happen to her, and she cried a little when her coworkers showed up with gifts for her, too.

"For Piper, who's always working too hard," Gloria said, thrusting a wrapped package into her hands.

"For Piper, who won't let me steal cupcakes anymore," Whitney said, handing her a package too. Piper sniffled.

"You're all too nice. I don't know what to say."

Whitney dropped her voice. "It's a gift for Lyra, too, but... just don't open it here."

Piper paled. "Whitney, did you get us..."

"We're so proud of you doing this," Gloria said, puling her into a hug. "I missed these kinds of events."

It was a fun event, too, I had to admit. Laughter filled the air as people ate, drank, and danced, people who hadn't been in town in years recounting old stories. My favorite sight, though, was how Piper's eyes shone as she looked out over it all, welling up with pride—pride for this thing she'd dreamed up out of nothing and made into reality. I caught her by the side of the room looking out over it all like towards the end of the event, and I looped an arm around her waist.

"I'm proud of you," I said.

"Thanks. I'm proud of you too." She paused. "What are we proud of me for?"

I gestured to the floor. "Looks like you were right. Maybe there is still hope for Christmas in Castle Hollow."

She laughed, eyes sparkling. "Oh, Lyra. Just you wait and see. The festival's still coming. You haven't seen nothing yet." She offered me a hand. "It's getting late. Let's go steal the show and dance."

We stole the show. No doubt about it—she took me to the center of the floor and danced, swirling to the music, our feet flowing in time even when Piper stumbled, and people stepped back to give us space at the center, right before the Christmas tree. It felt like we were on a stage, a captive audience gathered around, and my heart pounded wildly in my chest no matter how much I tried to look cool.

If Piper felt so alive because of that purpose, that meaning she had in her life, then this? This felt like purpose. Meaning. More than I was used to finding in my day-to-day.

And it made me want more.

When we finished the dance, Piper didn't hesitate—she fell against me, threw her arms around my neck, and kissed me like the wild, free spirit she was, and I held her by the waist and kissed her back. The crowds cheered and clapped around us, and I heard Gloria shouting something about *that's our Christmas Committee* that I would think about later, and I heard Louisa gushing to Charlie about how cute we were—heard the chorused cheers from Whitney and Ethan and Bella and Herman and Colin and Rose and all the other people I'd gotten to meet over the whirlwind since I'd gotten to Castle Hollow—and I wanted to wrap myself up in this feeling.

And when the cheering subsided, it faded down to just one person clapping. Piper and I stepped back from one another, turning to where the crowds parted and people gasped softly, murmured amongst themselves as an older man stepped through the crowds toward us, a kindly smile on his face, wispy white hair a little patchy on top of his head. Piper straightened next to me, her lips parting.

"Fredrik Walton?" she said. The old man—Castle Hollow's former Father Christmas—smiled wider, eyes crinkling.

"You did good, Piper."

Chapter 13

PIPER

The hall fell into a shocked silence, almost reverent. I couldn't blame them. What were you supposed to say at a time like this? I stood there gobsmacked at best, flabbergasted at worst. Was there a difference? I didn't know, but if there was, I was probably both.

"Oh my god, it's been so long," I said, finally, stepping forwards and holding my arms out for a hug. "We thought you were never coming back here! My mom told me you'd gone off to work at Santa's workshop. You came back?"

"I heard tell about you and your girlfriend picking things up around here," he said, looking between me and Lyra. "You know something, Piper, I always thought I'd find you like this."

I hunched my shoulders. "You... give me too much credit. I'm nothing special. I only did this with a lot of help."

"Oh?" He shook his head. "Oh, I meant—I always thought you'd end up with a girlfriend, more than anything else."

"Oh my god." I put a hand to my forehead. "Yeah... well, you got me!"

"But it's true too, you always did know what Christmas at Castle Hollow was all about. Mayor Bolton told me about you—running the cultural committee all by yourself, making this place matter to people. If anyone was going to take over after me, I know you were the right choice." He smiled wider, shoving his hands in his pockets. "You really made something special here, Piper."

"Oh, stop it. I can't handle too many compliments. My girlfriend already gives me so many. She's really nice."

He laughed, that familiar old chuckle I really thought I'd never hear again. My mind was racing—full of dreams that maybe this was the turning point for Castle Hollow. "It's really something," he said. "That's why I'm here. I'm ready for a real Christmas festival, just like the ones Castle Hollow used to have."

"Yes!" I clapped my hands together. "Yes, I'm *so* ready. I've been waiting so long to do this!"

"I have the space, the resources, everything planned out," he said, and then the pin bursting the balloon that had been my excitement getting too big and rising too high, he said, "right in Madison."

I stiffened. A murmur went through the crowds. I pursed my lips. "Are you... just inviting us to the city's Christmas festival?"

"Of course! There's so many people there ready to ring in Christmas. It's already been lit up beautifully all month, and walking through those streets, you'd swear it's just like Castle Hollow of old. I know it's a drive," he said, putting a hand up, "but if you're already driving fifteen minutes to get into town for the celebration, what's an extra forty once in the year to experience Christmas like we all dream of?"

"What—but—" My stomach dropped. That was nothing alike. That was—touring for a Christmas event in another place. Compared to stepping outside and seeing it out your front door, living in the dream every day—*that* was what Fredrik Walton came up with as his dream to bring back to us?

"I'll be there," Ethan said, stepping up from the crowd. "The wife and I love a big Christmas bash. I'd love to see one really put together right."

"But—" I started, but my mom's friend Anna stepped forward too.

"I can't wait to see it," she said. "When is it?"

"The twentieth," Fredrik said, and my blood ran cold—the same day *our* festival was supposed to be. The day the tourism board was coming through.

"I'll be there," another voice said. Bella chimed in, "I'm ready to see a Fredrik Walton Christmas again," but that was when Lyra stepped up next to me and put a hand on my back.

"You won't," she said, looking at Bella. "Mr. Walton here hasn't had any hand in the festivities at Madison."

Another murmur went through the crowd. I got a nervous flush as I looked over at her. "Lyra?"

She turned back to Fredrik. "Am I wrong, Mr. Walton? Or am I wrong to believe that you're working directly for Michael Landgrave, who's getting your help in sabotaging the Castle Hollow festival on the day the tourism board is coming through? I daresay it seems more likely he's the one who organized all of this—including your Christmas party in Madison."

Fredrik just smiled that sweet old smile he had, and I couldn't wrap my mind around all this coming from *him* of all people. "Makes me happy to see the young folks sticking up for Castle Hollow," he said. "But there's no sense lying to the tourism board. Let the people of the town decide if they want to go through the work of setting up something that's less popular every year, or make a once-a-year event out of going and experiencing it larger than life. We shouldn't be so ashamed of Castle Hollow as it really is that we're covering it up for the tourism board to come through."

"Yeah," Ethan said, although he looked visibly uncomfortable now. "Let's just let that happen. I'm happy with Castle Hollow as it is."

Lyra frowned. "You're very slick with the way you put these things, Mr. Walton. Let's analyze the facts clearly. Do you, or do you not, work for Michael Landgrave of Landgrave Estates?"

Fredrik waved her off. "Please. We can set aside rivalries for Christmas—"

"If you won't answer the question, Mr. Walton, we can assume you do work for Landgrave—and furthermore that you acknowledge it as a shameful thing to hide from us. Next question. Is Mr. Landgrave attempting to purchase the land along the Castle Hollow town center for his real estate developments, or is he not?"

Fredrik furrowed his brow, and he turned to the people all gathered around instead. "Do we want to hear an investigation, or do we want to have a Christmas party? Come on, everyone. Let's—"

I cut in. "I'm not going to the festival in Madison, Fredrik."

He turned back to me. I swallowed past the lump in my throat.

"I think it's a little suspect you won't answer any of Lyra's questions. Is it because you want to disrupt Castle Hollow's cultural grant and convince us to sell to Landgrave? Because the timing is a little suspicious too."

Fredrik just shook his head, a sad smile on his features. "If you don't want to come, Piper, we'll miss you terribly. It's going to be just like the festival as we knew it—back in the happier days of this town. But I don't want to taint this celebration with arguments and accusations. For everyone who wants to join us for a real Christmas celebration... I'll see you in Madison."

It broke my heart when people cheered for it, following along after him to thank him for coming, to talk to him, ask questions, so many things until it was just me and Lyra and a slim handful of other people left behind. A metaphor for something I didn't want to think about.

Mom sidled up next to me. "Who was that?"

I sighed. "Just some guy."

Olive slouched from the side of the room, iced coffee in hand. "Hey. I'm here. What'd I miss?"

"Everything, Olive." I sighed, my shoulders sinking. Lyra wrapped an arm tighter around my waist.

"We should probably head home," she said. "It's getting late. The cleanup crew will be coming through soon..."

"Yeah. Guess you're right." I turned back to where Gloria was giving me a sad smile, and I could see it all there—*you did your best*. Maybe that was it.

What were you supposed to do when your best wasn't good enough?

I didn't say a word the whole drive back to my house. Lyra got ready for bed right alongside me without me even having to ask, and at least when I lay sleepless in bed that night, I got to feel Lyra's warmth on the bed next to me, got to hear her slow breaths in and out.

The cleanup crew took care of everything in the community center. The decorations stayed up, but the rest of the party was hollowed out, until it was just a reminder that I'd believed in Christmas miracles for a minute.

I went to work the next morning, and we all worked in a solemn quiet. I mean—except for Beck. He still listened to his bossa nova a little too loud on his headphones, jamming along while he put together Excel spreadsheets and not using nearly enough keyboard shortcuts. Herman, normally full of life and laughter when he came in for a minute to pick up his stuff and head out for errands, walked like it was a funeral procession. *Feliz Navidad* on the overhead speaker felt too happy for the mood. I didn't *want* to have a feliz Navidad. I was going to have an... unfeliz Navidad if I so felt like it.

And with the way things were going, I was going to lose my job, the town was going to lose its chance at making Christmas magic, and Lyra was going to leave me. That sounded pretty unfeliz a Navidad to me.

When I got back to my house after work, Lyra wasn't there. She'd left a note on the kitchen table saying she was having some emergency video meetings for work and was taking them back at the rental house, but the note was at least attached to a box of Christmas cookies from the bakery and it said to help myself, so I sat wrapped up in a blanket watching Rudolph and eating Christmas cookies all by myself like a loser.

I was still wrapped up in blankets with a few too many cookie crumbs on myself when there was a knock at the door, and I opened the door in my bunny-printed onesie and found Lyra there, her expression drawn taut.

"Hi," she said. "Sorry to bother you. Just... wanted to talk."

"The meetings were that bad?" I stepped back to let her in, and she hugged herself tightly as she stepped in out of the cold and took off her shoes.

"They certainly weren't good."

"What's wrong?" I shook my head. "No, don't tell me. You look awful. Why don't you sit down and wrap up in a blanket and eat a cookie while I make you tea and then we can talk?"

She sighed. "You don't need to do all that—"

"I want to. It's part of my work as the head of the cultural committee."

She flashed a smile at me. "You are a special woman, Piper. Thank you."

Not special enough to make anyone care about Christmas here after all, but I could at least make tea. I had that one down.

Two minutes later, though, I spilled hot water on the counter, so clearly I didn't have that one down after all. Lyra asked if I was okay, calling from the next room when I gasped and mopped up the spill.

"I'm fine! Just clumsy. Everything's fine. Tea is on its way."

When I sat on the couch, I hunched over myself, and Lyra draped the blanket over both of us, wrapping an arm around me. "You didn't burn yourself on the water, did you?"

"The way you immediately know that I spilled." I shook my head. "No, just the counter. I cleaned it up. We're good."

She sighed. "My boss is giving me a suspension."

I turned to her. "A—what? Is that like a suspension from school?"

"He doesn't have a fireable offense on record for me, and I'm protected by a good union, so he can't get rid of me outright, but I'm losing him money. So he's essentially giving me unpaid time off and telling me I have to take it until things cool down."

My chest ached, and I squeezed her arm. "That's awful. Are you going to be okay?"

"I'll be fine for now... I have plenty of savings." She looked away. "And I won't be suspended for long if I do as I'm told and jump through the hoops right."

"What hoops? What's happening?"

She sank back in her seat, turning and looking at the Christmas tree with a pensive stare. "It's Landgrave. He's been defaming me. He was running cold inquiries into me for a while, and I thought it was just him looking for dirt, but it turns out he's been circulating a rumor I'm involved in illegal work and that's why there's so many inquiries into me. It doesn't hold up under any serious investigation, but that doesn't matter when people respond with a kneejerk and don't seriously investigate. Clients have been refusing to work with us as long as I'm on board, so... my boss told me to disappear until I'm ready to suck up to Landgrave instead and get this sorted."

I was going to cry. Her words stuck in my chest like little barbs until I wanted to shrink into myself, curl up into a little ball and vanish. "You're in all this trouble and it's my fault."

"Hey. Piper." She put a hand on my back, but I pushed her away.

"No, don't try to reassure me. I've set these ridiculous pie-in-the-sky goals, and now I've dragged you down with me. I was so sure of myself, and then I screwed up, and now my job, Castle Hollow, your job, even—"

She kissed me. I grunted, but I didn't fight it—just froze up for a second before I sank into her, let it happen, let the warmth of her lips melt against mine.

When she pulled away, I said, "Oh... huh."

"What?"

I laughed breathlessly. "Oh my god, we did the thing."

"What thing?"

"The whole—kissing her in the middle of an argument thing." I touched my lips. "That's cute."

She sighed, a smile on her lips as she squeezed my arm. "Piper. I don't want you to blame yourself. I walked into all of this willingly. And if I wanted to, I could turn around and leave all this behind right now, suck up to Landgrave and get my job back. I'm here because I want to be. Trust in that."

I hunched my shoulders, looking down. "You're one to lecture me about self-sacrifice. You shouldn't have to throw all of that away just for somebody else's sake."

"Maybe." But she didn't pull away, staying there with her arm on my back, her side warm against mine. After a minute, I swallowed.

"If you're going to be here at least for now... do you want to make something nice for dinner? Put on a fire, watch a movie?"

"I'd love that. Anything to take my mind off Landgrave for right now."

It did help, just a little—heading into the kitchen and putting on music while we made a rich pumpkin and sage soup, sitting together on the couch all wrapped up in our blanket sharing soup, the fireplace crackling while a movie played on the TV. Once the credits rolled and we scraped the last soup from our bowls, spoons scratching on the rough ceramic, I sank against Lyra, and she wrapped me up in her arms and lowered onto her back, holding me against her chest. I listened to the sound of her heartbeat, watching as snowflakes drifted against the windowsill, feeling her warmth wrapping me up.

"Lyra," I said, my voice small and scratchy. She stroked my hair back.

"Yes, Piper?"

"What do you think I'm supposed to do?"

She hummed quietly to herself. "Well," she said, "what do you want to happen?"

I chewed my lip. "Am I supposed to be realistic?"

"No."

"I want a hundred billion dollars and a pet unicorn."

She hummed again. "Maybe just *slightly* realistic."

I buried my face against her collar. "Fine. I want the town to be like it used to be. I want to throw a big Christmas festival here just like the ones it used to have, but it's more than just Christmas. I want my friends to come back. I want this town to feel like it has a future. To feel like it has people in it. And..."

And I wish I could tell all those people you were my girlfriend for real. But some things died on my lips, words too meaningful to be spoken. She squeezed me.

"Then I guess you fight for it, huh?"

"Who do I fight? I'll punch them out."

"I'm sure you'd do great, sweetie, but maybe less literally. Let's throw a festival."

I paused. "You mean that? *Here?*"

"That was the plan, wasn't it?"

"But—no one's going to show up." I pushed myself up to sitting. "You heard everyone at the dance. They're all eager to go see whatever Fredrik Walton is doing in Madison. No one's going to be going to *our* sorry little festival held together by duct tape and a dream."

"Or," she said, measuring her words carefully, "maybe they will, once they realize how much you care about it."

I laughed drily, only then realizing there were tears hanging on the edges of my vision. "Look at you, being all mushy now. Like we can do this with the power of love?"

"Do I look like a Saturday morning cartoon character?" She shook her head. "Here's what I think. I think everyone is waiting around wishing somebody else would take that step to make this town like it used to be. But none of them really believe it's possible."

"I've been trying all this time..."

"You've been *working* all this time. But when you just take on whatever everybody around you wants you to do, you end up going in circles. Were you really going to get any time to focus on throwing the festival this year, or were you going to get sucked into doing Whitney's mail?"

I didn't say anything. She stroked my hair back, and I... never realized how calming that was until just now. I wanted her to keep doing it forever.

"I've heard it from Gloria, from your mother, from Ethan and Bella and everyone you've introduced me to—they're all wishing it would go back to the way it was. I don't think you need to change the town singlehandedly. I think you just need to show them that it is possible."

I sniffled, a hot feeling in my throat. "But… it's… I've never managed it before."

"We all need someone to believe in us." She tucked a lock of hair back behind my ear, smiling slyly. "And despite my initial misgivings—I definitely believe in you, Piper. The helper needs help too. I'll do what I can to pitch in."

"But—your job—your everything," I said, my voice wavering.

"I'm thinking…" She chewed her lip. "Maybe I could go back downtown and suck up to Landgrave and his buddies to get back in the clear. Or… maybe I could help you and the rest of the town hall fight off Landgrave, and make my own name for myself without kissing ass to get there. If I can do that, my firm's going to have to *bid* to get me back."

I stared at her for the longest time, a sudden nervous feeling making my heart pound. "You mean… you're going to stay and help?"

"At least through however long Landgrave is going to keep going at it. I'll bet he's throwing all his resources into the fight before Christmas, anyway, so it's no extra time." She smiled wryly.

"But if I had to stay a little longer... it's not like it's terrible sticking around with my sugarsquish."

"Oh my god. Lyra! Pulling something like that out now." I laughed through tears, and I buried my face in my hands. She pulled me into an embrace, and I nestled against her collar. "You really think I have any chance—"

"Hey, you told me yourself. You don't even know the meaning of the word failure." She ruffled my hair. "You didn't go learning a new word, did you? I'm sure your sister would be appalled."

I laughed. How it was that Lyra fit so easily into my life, into my world, I didn't know. But if she put it all on the line to help me save Castle Hollow and *then* left—I couldn't imagine how much that would break my heart.

But maybe then there would be a little bit of Lyra in all the happy memories around Castle Hollow. And that would have to be good enough for me.

"Okay," I said. "Let's... let's do it. A festival that'll blow Uptown Mikey out of the water." I squeezed her tighter. "Or maybe *into* the water. Into a freezing lake. With cactuses up his ass."

"I wouldn't have it any other way, Piper."

I had a good not-girlfriend on my side.

Chapter 14
LYRA

We set up for the festival.

In a way, I think it was a blessing I got shadow-fired. Without my mornings taken up by contracts, I got to throw myself headfirst into helping Piper, who picked herself up again after a nice long cry and a good night's sleep. She was back to her radiant self again in the morning, when she came down two hours after I'd woken up, kicked open the door into the kitchen, shoved me against the counter and kissed me.

I wasn't complaining about that kind of good-morning greeting.

We started with canvasing, visiting a dozen different houses and arguing with people to set up stalls for the festival, to help with cleaning up, fixing up, and prettying up the town center. One no after another shook Piper, but like clockwork, the girl just needed a cookie and a coffee and she was back to full steam ahead.

We got off to a rocky start—three full days and no progress—but I had a breakthrough when I caught Gloria at the town hall, cornering her behind the Christmas tree and next to a wall of

Rudolphs and thrusting a booklet of papers into her hands.

"I'm looking for ownership information and rental availability of all these units."

She took the papers, putting on bifocals from her desk and leafing through them. "You lawyers really do live fancy lives, if you want to just rent all of these on a whim."

"For the last time, I'm not a lawyer. They're not for *me,* Gloria. Just get me the information."

She tapped away at her computer for a bit before it was clear she wasn't getting anything on the computer, and she took me to rows of filing cabinets that Piper—bless her beautiful soul— had meticulously decorated in tinsel and lights, a red ribbon on each drawer handle. A few minutes later, I had a sea of papers, and I scanned them quickly.

"All right. Let's claim them all."

"Er—" She scratched her head. "Eminent domain is pretty passé these days."

"These units have all been empty for at least five years, and property values are declining. They're just property tax sinks for the owners, and are too tax-expensive to just unload. Let's just offer tax-reduced escapes to the owners, see how many we can claim."

She laughed. "I don't understand at all, but *you* definitely do. You're more like Piper than I realized. You both get these wild ideas and you turn into little balls of fire. Am I ever glad she found a sexy lesbian lawyer."

"Gloria, once again, I am not a lawyer." I paused. "Or a lesbian, for that matter."

It was four hours of calls later that I finally crashed on the desk, just as Piper came into the town hall with a box of donuts. "Christmas pastries," she called, and she went wide-eyed at the sight of me face-first flat on the desk. "Oh, god, my girlfriend's dead."

"Just feel like it. I hate phone calls."

Whitney swept in out of nowhere, which was terrifying because I didn't even know she was *in* today and I'd been here for the past five hours, and she took a donut from the box. "Thanks, Piper," she said. "You and Lyra gotten any use from your gift yet?"

Piper sighed, turning back to me. "You okay, Lyra?"

"I'm good. Just scoring free property."

"Oh. Uptown Mikey's gonna be jealous."

I sat up straighter, snatching a donut from the box and taking the cup of medium-roast coffee she got me. "I'm collecting potential transfers to get the shopping center back, along with the strip in the town center. It got sold off piecemeal to private speculators years ago, and I'm going to propose some legal maneuvers from the township so Mayor Bolton can get them back for free."

"Oh... I just got you donuts, and you bought me a mall. I've lost Christmas gifting this year."

I smiled dryly. "There is no beating donuts. I'm not just collecting a mall for interest's sake. I happen to know quite a few people back in Chicago who would be interested in free commercial real estate just in time for a townwide festival with the state tourism board coming through, all in exchange just for fixing the place up a little."

Piper dropped her arms by her sides, staring with lips parted. "You—are you actually, honest-to-god reinventing the *mall* in this century?"

"A place for people to gather is a timeless concept. A place for people to spend money while they gather is a timeless concept under capitalism. Think you know any friends who would be interested in renting like that?"

She laughed breathlessly. "My... friends?"

"Anyone who's moved out of town. We have to have *some* unique value proposition to draw them back in."

"Oh my god, you're really doing this."

I gestured to my phone. "Would I have spent four hours on the phone if I weren't?"

She leaned over the desk, cupped my head in both hands, and kissed me fiercely. I grunted, hands going up, and I heard Gloria behind me making that sound where I just *knew* she was dramatically fanning herself, but I kissed Piper back. Her eyes were sparkling as she pulled away again. "You are the absolute best girlfriend ever," she said, and I wasn't really sure if she meant it as part of the act or not.

Well, I knew full well what the answer was. I was just afraid of the answer.

"I try my best to keep up with you, but there's no beating donuts," I said.

"So! We're talking to investors, to Mayor Bolton, and to potential commercial real estate buyers—"

"Why do I get the feeling *we* are talking to them today?"

"Because you've learned how Piper time works. C'mon! I can take over phone calls. I like talking to people. We're better as a team."

No doubt, she was right about that one.

It took another two days of almost nonstop calls and video meetings, which was my anathema, but we'd gotten back a good half of the old mall and the shopping strip in the town center—including all the space we needed to extend the festival indoors. Convincing buyers was the harder part. A dozen people I knew from Chicago were interested only to open a franchise location or something similar, but Piper and I vetoed every suggestion for it, and it looked like hopes were running thin over the next two days until, finally, one person agreed to use an old space to open a specialty funnel cake popup shop.

I put down the phone and sighed, falling backwards on Piper's couch. She looked up from where she was typing furiously on her laptop.

"Someone said yes," I said. She lit up, jaw dropping before shifting into a massive smile.

"We got one?"

"A specialty funnel cake popup shop."

She paused. "Um... cool! That's... new."

"I responded more tactfully, but that was the exact response I had on the inside."

She clapped her hands together. "Oh my god, I can't wait to try some specialty funnel cake. I bet the tourism board will love that."

"I'll buy you the raspberry-pistachio. They said that's their favorite."

She raised her eyebrows. "A bit fancy for a funnel cake, don't you think?"

"I thought so too. Clearly we just don't know specialty funnel cake."

But no matter who it was, it helped. Funnel cake guy was our proof of concept, and saying we already had a buyer in one space greased the wheels for other buyers. Someone who wanted a physical space for a small team's handcrafted jewelry signed up, and then a clothing boutique, and then a sandwich shop—all just popup shops, but they'd have to do for now.

It was the next morning, when I was out to meet a new tenant and grab coffee for me and Piper on the way back, when I found Bella Burnes with a posse of older women making their way through the town center, each carrying a massive box of holly and wreaths. When I saw her stop to hang up a wreath on a signpost on one of the shuttered shopfronts in the main commercial strip—now with a sign saying *Opening Soon* instead of *For Sale*—I found myself drawn to her, standing nearby and clearing my throat. She whirled, eyes wide.

"Oh! Oh, it's Piper's girlfriend." She came over and offered me a hug, and I'd figured out that was just how things worked around here, so I hugged her. "Good morning, Lyra. It's so early to be out and about. Sun's barely up, you know. What are you doing?"

"I'm going to a meeting. Nothing interesting. What's more interesting is why *you* are out and about this early, you and your friends."

She put her hands on her hips, beaming. "This is my gardening club! Sam talked at the last meeting about how you and your girlfriend are getting the town center opened back up for the festival—and maybe even keeping it open—and so I told them, well, *that* won't do, not without some damn Christmas cheer."

I paused. "We... were planning on hiring decorators—"

"Oh, forget that. Call someone in from out of town to tell us how to pretty the place up for Christmas? *Us?* No one tells Castle Hollow how to do Christmas. Not even Fredrik Walton. Leave your decorators out of this. My girls and I will get this place ready for Christmas."

I think that was the point it finally settled in— Piper was right. She'd been right all along, bless her beautiful, bright-eyed soul.

This town was just *waiting* to celebrate Christmas.

"Perfect," I said. "I'll be counting on you. Let me and Piper know how we can support you all, all right? We're in this together."

Bella's eyes crinkled as she smiled. "Nice to be part of a community again. I can't wait for the festival."

Neither could I.

It came together in a miracle over the next week. An impromptu street crew to fix up the old infrastructure in places, half the town joining in decorations crews, often with their own handcrafted decorations, and a proper full-sized Christmas tree finally going up in the town center. I think we got about every resident in town together to help decorate the tree on a cold evening speckled with snow flurries—even Olive begrudgingly tying in boughs of tinsel at the lowest level. When Piper told Mayor Bolton to put the star at the top of the tree, a crowd booed before he could say a word, and by enormous peer pressure, Piper ended up climbing the ladder alongside me to put a big, lit-up star at the top of the tree, to the cheers of the crowds.

"I know I love attention and all," Piper whispered as cameras flashed from below, "but, um... do you think maybe they mistook me for someone actually important?"

"No," I laughed, "I think they have exactly the right idea."

"Okay, cool. Well, I'll just collect the bouts of impostor's syndrome, hang them up on my wall..."

This girl had nothing to feel like an impostor over, genius that she was.

The shopping center filled up, too—a whole wild collection of niche shops, all working around spaces that were a little run-down in places, but the small-town charm of the strip with all its odd shops was undeniable. Christmas music played loud through the main street, and stalls went up in the town center in preparation for the festival. In the few days leading up to the event, Piper and I couldn't step out of the town hall without her gushing over running into someone she'd known from years back—people taking extended trips back to Castle Hollow for Christmas, or even some trying their hand at opening a shop in the cheap real estate to impress the tourism board. Who knew where they all came from. Piper just had a *lot* of friends.

What I did know, though, was that this place was nothing like the sad little forgotten town I'd found when I'd shown up. The streets bustling, shops opening, music filling the air as people ran into old friends in the street—it was looking a lot more like Piper had described it.

It was such a rush that I lost track of time, and I didn't know what was happening until the day before the festival, when Gloria called me and Piper into the town hall office—we'd been a bit too busy to stop in for regular affairs there lately—and we arrived to find a surprise party, party poppers going off when we stepped inside, the employees there along with Piper's family and a handful of others.

"Oh my god," Piper said, hands to her chest. "As if we didn't have enough parties lately?"

I elbowed her. "Who are you and what have you done with Piper, that you're implying such a thing as *too many parties?*"

"I just—I'm not important enough for this many parties!" she protested, red-faced as the other town hall employees gathered around us.

"Balderdash," Gloria said. "The only reason any of this is happening is because of you and your sexy lawyer girlfriend."

"For the last time," I started.

Whitney piped up. "I even canceled all my tickets to the Madison event. I was planning on buying them all up and then reselling them for twice the price, but now I don't think anyone's interested…"

Piper put a hand to her chest. "Whitney. You were price-gouging off our potential downfall?"

"Sure was. Gotta take the opportunity where you get it."

Louisa, who had been struggling with her party popper for a solid two minutes, finally set it off. She cheered as if Piper had just walked in the door, and everyone else had the decency to cheer with her again.

But we gathered around the breakroom table and cut slices of cake for us, and Piper and I sat so close we were practically in the same chair, sharing one double-size slice of cake at Gloria's insistence. Piper teared up a little when she picked up her fork, though, staring down at the cake before she put her fork down and buried her face in her hands. I put a hand on her back.

"Angel?" I said softly. The pet names had been coming more and more naturally lately. I wondered if I was supposed to be worried about that. "What's wrong?"

"It's a really pretty cake," she said, voice barely there through tears. "I don't want to destroy it."

"It's very lovely," I said, "but it *is* a plain white cake with no decorations. And I seem to recall you saying something about how pretty things are meant to be destroyed. Any chance this is something else?"

She shook her head, wiping her eyes. "Sorry, everyone. Just... thank you. I don't know if I really... stopped to ever think maybe this could really happen. I've been really happy to see Castle Hollow... like I remember it."

Louisa lit up. "Oh! Is that why we're here?"

Charles put a hand on her back. "Yes, darling. The festival is tomorrow."

"What festival?"

Charles rubbed his chin. "Actually, I'm not sure I remember..."

I cleared my throat. "Piper—"

But the door unlatched and swung open before I could say anything else, and stomping snow into the building, huddled in a big coat, the stringy figure of Michael Landgrave came storming into the room, an icy wind sweeping in behind him. Everyone stopped, looking up at him, and he shook the snow from his coat.

"Merry Christmas to all of you," he said. "My good friends of Castle Hollow—Mr. Walton sent some gifts."

I shot him a withering look. "Nice to finally meet you in person, Mister Landgrave," I said. "I know you've been making so many inquiries into me, you must have been *very* curious about who I am. Now you finally get to meet me and put all your questions to rest."

Louisa cocked her head. "What kind of gifts?"

Landgrave helped himself to a seat across from me and Piper, unbuttoning his coat down to a blazer. "I thought I'd come here and congratulate you all. You've really had a little... renaissance with this town, haven't you? Just wanted to warn you it's not a smart idea to play so fast and loose with real estate law."

The tears and softness in Piper's expression were gone all at once, replaced with a burning intensity, her lips drawn in a tight line, and she stood up, her arms folded. "Really, really bold of you," she said, "to try that on the girl who's dating a real estate lawyer."

I wasn't a lawyer, but now wasn't the time for that. Landgrave took it, though, scoffing in my direction.

"Lyra Simmons is no lawyer. Contract writer at best—*former* contract writer, I should say. Or didn't you know?" He sat up straighter. "Suspended from her work at a legal firm for her suspected ties to accounting fraud in commercial real estate, and run out here to Castle Hollow to lay low. How much vetting did you all give her? How much of your real estate transactions did you trust her with?"

The room looked to me, and I fought down the sick feeling in my throat. I couldn't believe this was what he'd been planning—at most maybe a desperate move when he realized he was outplayed. But I was getting sick of false rumors, whether it was about cheating or accounting fraud. "Mister Landgrave," I started, but he cut in.

"Where were the accounting reports for the reclamation of the whole shopping strip, the mall, everything? Smash and grab wholesale stripping everything just for a chance to consolidate, a common real estate shark using *goodwill* for the town hall as a pretty little cover story. Or did you think I wasn't paying attention to what you did in sleepy little Castle Hollow?" He stood up. "No matter what all of you do, *I* care about this town. And I know it has the potential to become home to so many people. A vibrant community, connected by a shared purpose—"

"Stop talking."

It was Piper who stilled the room with two words, spoken in that way that said *there's no disagreeing with me on this.* Landgrave flinched, but he went silent for that crucial second where Piper commanded the room. Slowly, she stood.

Landgrave spoke up. "I don't know what you and Lyra have—"

"Listen to yourself." Piper's voice was almost *scolding* now, like a disappointed mother. He flinched again. "You're lying through your teeth, and you know it full well. Do you think you're going to get anywhere like that? Do you think a single person in this room believes you?"

He stood up too, red-faced now—furious, no doubt, at the *audacity* of a smaller, pretty woman to contradict him. "It doesn't matter who believes me or not. What matters is that I already have a team of legal experts who are combing through every one of your shady conglomeration acquisitions as we speak, and before you know it, they're going to drag you in for—"

"For what, Mister Landgrave?" I said. "Compliance fees over untimely reporting? What we did was completely legal, and you know it. If the worst you can find is some late documents—"

"The reputation of this entire town—" Landgrave started, but Piper shook her head.

"I think the tourism board will like what they see tomorrow. And I don't think they're going to do any good for the *reputation* of someone trying to tear it down for the suburb of a company park." She planted her hands on the table, leaning forward. "Do a thorough cost-benefit analysis. You've lost, and you look like a loser. You called in the tourism board, and we have all your plans for this place on record. If anyone comes to us talking about you, we have every document to show you were calling in the tourism board in an attempt to knock this place down, and they're going to choose us. This. You know they will. That's why you came here, because you're scared and you're desperate. You have two options. Either keep going and pushing a narrative about Lyra that can only damage her reputation for a few months at most, and have it fall apart on you—the rumors you put out about her, the sabotage you pulled on this town, the way you tried to pay off our festival in Madison instead— and crush *your* reputation..." She stood up straighter. "Or turn around, walk back out that door, and never, ever, *ever* come back. Oh, and shove a cactus up your ass. Third time's the charm."

Landgrave stood, white-faced now, gripping the edge of the table. Piper pointed at me.

"Also, she's *definitely* a lawyer. She graduated law school and writes legal documents. I don't get why this is so hard for everyone! That's one hundred percent lawyer territory!"

Landgrave banged a fist on the table. "If this is what you want—if you're all deciding to side with a disgraced legal intern like Lyra—"

"I'm siding with her," Piper said. "Everyone in this room is siding with her."

Gloria stood up. "*I'm* siding with Lyra. Everyone in this *town* is siding with Lyra! She's a member of Castle Hollow now. We trust her more than your cactus-stuffed ass."

Beck, who had been sitting in the corner the whole time, put his hand up. "I trust Lyra. She's got the right vibes."

"I know we trust Lyra," Charles said. "If my darling Louisa trusts her, I trust her. She's a perfect girlfriend to my precious little daughter."

Louisa cocked her head. "Hold on. I'm a little confused. Who's he? Are he and Piper mad at each other? If so, then he's definitely wrong. My daughter would never be wrong."

Whitney, who hadn't stopped eating her cake the whole time, spoke through a mouthful. "Better listen to Piper. This is her territory. If she says Lyra stays, Lyra stays."

I relaxed, giving Landgrave a small smile. "You heard them," I said. "Looks like your little smear campaign can only go so far. Seems they've taken a liking to me. Besides, I, uh... I'm quite partial to my girlfriend."

Landgrave stepped back, his lips drawn in a tight line. Finally, he shook his head, spun on his heel, and marched back towards the door. "Do what you like, then," he said. "See if I care what happens to your sorry little town. I have better prospects to move onto."

He stormed out, and he slammed the door behind him. We fell into silence, all just watching the door—waiting, like we were afraid he might burst back in and start again—before finally, Piper laughed.

"That was cathartic," she said, falling back into her chair. "I need to yell at smartasses more often. That felt great."

I laughed, putting my hand down on top of hers. It felt as natural as if there had never been an *act* to keep up in the first place. "I'd love to be party to that," I said. "It's satisfying to watch."

She turned to me, eyes sparkling. "You are so good for my ego. I've got to keep you around."

I was dangerously tempted to let her do just that. I picked up a forkful of cake. "Merry Christmas, Piper."

"Merry Christmas—"

I put the cake in her mouth, and she let out a muffled grunt around it. Somehow, that marked the moment for everyone to let go of the tension that had been thick through the room, and Gloria stood up, cheering. Piper's parents clapped, and the room lit up in a festive glow.

"—Lyra," Piper finished, after swallowing the cake, smiling at me, eyes shining.

I really *was* tempted.

Chapter 15

PIPER

The festival was just like I remembered it. I'd missed Castle Hollow—*this* Castle Hollow, where I got to walk down the main street, through the stalls, smelling Jonathan's traditional candied orange peel recipe and the marbled hot chocolate from the Bard family, their five-year-old daughter attending the festival for the first time, looking around at the lights and the crowds like it was the most magical thing she'd ever seen. I remembered when that had been me.

And this time, I got to walk through it all hand-in-hand with Lyra Simmons, who I was falling for harder every day.

After a whole month of working so hard to put everything together, working desperately to keep the town alive, getting to just walk through the brisk winter air and take it all in—going shopping at a collection of odd popup shops and traditional family-style stalls, trying foods new and familiar, talking and laughing the whole time with Lyra, it made me feel whole in a way I didn't know how to handle. Like all these little pieces I'd been realizing over the past month that I was missing, suddenly they were all in place, and I just swelled up with the feeling so much I thought I might cry.

We met the tourism board representatives at the specialty funnel cake shop, of all places, and they shook our hands warmly and gushed over how cozy and charming the festival was. When I introduced myself and Lyra to the lead, a tall and slender woman named Nadeesha, she smiled warmly at the two of us.

"I've heard of you. You're the town's Christmas Committee, right?"

"Oh, um..." I looked over at Lyra, and she laughed, putting a hand on my back and pulling me closer.

"That's us," she said. "And girlfriends, too."

I don't know if I fluttered more over Lyra finally agreeing on her own terms to be Christmas Committee after all or over her calling us *girlfriends*, even after Uptown Mikey was out of the picture.

Yeah, it was more over the girlfriends thing. But still! Christmas Committee! A girl could be excited about two things.

It was a dream touring the festival, ending up in a dance that went late into the night fueled by eggnog and a little brandy too, and heading home and sleeping late tangled up together before we went out for the next day of the festival. Three days of the festival blurred together into a swirl of dancing and laughing with friends, trying a whole collection of food and drink from weird and rare to familiar and comforting, and buying a long list of things we didn't need. Old friends I hadn't seen in years and years gushed to me about how much they loved the festival, all admitting secretly how much they missed Castle Hollow, and when Lyra and I told them to just move back here and not have to miss it at all, they almost looked convinced. Another year or two and I'd get to them, I knew. And I knew they'd be back next December, at least.

When I saw Katie again, along with her new boyfriend, I realized I'd definitely been admiring her in a gay way back in school. But I had a much prettier girl with me now anyway—a sexy lawyer, even. Even if she denied being one.

"And that's the thing," I said, laughing as Lyra and I danced up from the car back towards my house at the end of the third day, the festival all wrapped like waking up soft and content from a happy dream. "This is just the *first*. Next year we know what we're doing, we have the proof we can do it, we can start it earlier in the month and keep the celebrations going—and more people will be coming in—it'll be so beautiful. It's only getting better from here. Isn't that amazing?"

"It is," she said, and it took until we were inside and crashed on the couch together, my head resting against her collar, to realize that had lacked a whole lot of enthusiasm.

"Um... did you have fun?" I said, softly, suddenly dropping into anxious insecurity like the floor had given out from under me.

"A lot," she said, softly, trailing her fingers gently down my back. "Thank you. For letting me be a part. This has meant a lot."

My heart shattered like a delicate glass ornament. "You're... not going to leave too soon, are you?" I whispered, and she looked down.

"After it got out what happened with Landgrave, my boss wanted to reinstate me. At a... rather higher rate."

My insides were twisting up now, but I tried to force myself to look happy. I don't think I did well. "Oh... that's so great! So you get to have your job back..."

She sighed. "They want me working in-office as a representative. So... they want me back in Chicago."

Of course they wanted her. I couldn't blame them. I wanted her, too. "Well... I should congratulate you. I think that's just amazing. I'm sure you'll do great. Um... you're not leaving before Christmas, are you?"

It came out sounding a little too desperate. She sighed, hanging her head. "He wants to meet with me tomorrow."

I was going to cry. "Wow," I said, my voice scratchy. "You're, uh... in high demand, huh?"

She didn't say anything.

"No, I get it." I looked down. "You've been totally clear this whole time with what you wanted. And you've given me *so* much. This whole town couldn't have gotten through this without you. You helped me learn my own worth and stand up for myself. You, uh... helped me figure out I'm gay. Got me over the awkwardness around my first kiss. Um... I've loved every, *every* single second we've had together, you know. You're amazing. I just wish I could have you for real." My voice cracked, and I felt tears hot in my eyes no matter how much I tried to fight them. I shook my head, struggling to speak through it. "I'm sorry. I'm not supposed to say that part out loud. I'm not trying to impede on your success. I'll just miss you a *lot*. I've never felt like this about someone, Lyra."

She slipped an arm around my waist, pulling me into her. "I know. I'm... sorry. I don't want to leave this behind, but I don't think I can—"

"Please. Don't say all these words justifying it. They'll only hurt more." I buried my face in her shoulder, and she held me tightly into her. "I'm just... going to be happy I got to have you at all. You've made me really, really, really happy, Lyra. So happy I could cry. And I'll always remember you."

"Me too, Piper." She whispered the words softly in my ear. "I'm..." She shook her head with a sigh—trying not to say *I'm sorry* again, I was sure. I was glad. I couldn't take any *I'm sorry*. "For tonight, I'm all yours."

Tonight could never, ever, ever be enough. But I was just glad I got that much.

I was going to miss her a lot.

I faked smiles all through Christmas morning with my family. Cinnamon rolls for breakfast had been one of my favorite things, but now no number of cinnamon rolls were enough to pick me up. The cozy atmosphere in the air as we all sat on the floor in the living room and opened presents, bundled up in blankets and nightrobes against the chill in the air—it had been the coziest and sweetest and most nostalgic thing once, and now it just ached.

My parents both got me the exact same pair of slippers. They both laughed because they'd discussed who would buy those slippers, and apparently both forgot who they'd agreed would buy them, and both bought them, and they laughed and laughed, and I just forced a smile when normally I would have been laughing right along with them.

When they'd asked about Lyra, I'd just told them she had to be back in Chicago for work. It was *true,* even if it didn't cover the full reality of the situation. They'd been sad for about two minutes and then were right back to their usual selves, which was a relief—if they'd made a whole production of how sad it was, it would have broken me down further.

"Sorry," I said, after the gift-opening had turned into all sprawling on the floor talking about life, like we were all a bunch of kids. "I just have to run to the bathroom."

"Okay, sweetie," Mom said. "Oh, I might have—"

"Left the sink running, I know, I know."

She left the sink running. I turned it off. How did you even forget the sink running? It made sound.

I didn't really need to go to the bathroom. I just needed to close myself up in a room and scroll through pictures of me and Lyra on my phone—a million pictures I'd taken, mostly of Lyra looking at the camera in surprise or with a resigned smile on her face while I grinned like the camera was the best thing in the universe.

Suddenly I got why all the Christmas songs were either really happy or *really* wishing to be spending it with the one they cared about. Being lonely at Christmas hurt worse than anything I'd felt before, and one time I'd fallen down a staircase while carrying a coffee traveler and somehow managed to kick my shoe off my foot mid-fall and fling it into my own face. That had hurt a lot. Hurt my pride, too, since it had been at work and half a dozen people had seen it. But this hurt worse, because at least I knew the coffee burns would fade and my nose would stop being so red before long, but this? Maybe the ache would stop being so acute, but I didn't think I'd ever stop missing Lyra.

I spent a long time in the bathroom before I gathered my wits, and I went to flush the toilet so it sounded like I'd actually done something in the bathroom, but—my family wouldn't notice if I didn't. I could have fought a cat in the bathroom and they wouldn't notice. I stepped out of the bathroom, headed back downstairs, and I'd just sat back down to where they'd put on *Miracle on 34th Street*—as if I needed the reminder about when Lyra and I watched it together—when there was a knock at the door.

Mom looked up. "Was that the door?"

I turned to her. "Who are you expecting on Christmas?"

"Santa," she laughed, and she went back to the television.

"Um... Mom, Santa's not real." Another knock from the door. Nobody stirred. "Is nobody acknowledging the door knocking?"

"I'm sure it's just the mailman or something," Olive said. "Just chill."

"Olive, they don't deliver the mail on Christmas Day." Another knock. My heart suddenly pounded, and I stood up. "I'm... going to go get it."

Mom looked at me strangely. "Going to get what?"

I sighed. "Don't worry about it, okay, Mom? Enjoy your movie."

I pulled my robe tighter as I raced to the door, my heart pounding, wild fantasies flying through my mind, and—I psyched myself up at the door, suppressing all the nervous flutters, and I opened the door to where my neighbor Sarah handed me a wrapped package.

"Merry Christmas," she said. "This is from me and the husband. Sorry we forgot to get it to you earlier!"

"Oh..." I wanted to take her present and throw it in the snow. I smiled instead. "Thank you so much! This is lovely. Tell Nick I said thank you, too, okay? My parents and I really appreciate you two!"

She looked over my shoulder, an expectant smile on her face. "Where's the girlfriend?"

I was going to cry. I strained my smile. "Um... she's in the bathroom."

"Tell her I said hi, okay?"

I wouldn't. "I will."

I shut the door, and I leaned back against it for the longest time, just breathing slowly in and out and staring at the ceiling, and that was when I finally cried, just a little.

She really was gone. Just like that.

I headed back into the living room, and I set down the box on the coffee table. Mom looked at it funny. "Didn't we open all the presents already?"

"This is from Sarah. She says hi."

"Sarah? Sarah Millner? When was she here?"

I sighed. "Just now, Mom. That was her at the door."

"Which door?"

"Never mind that." Another knock, more timid, sheepish this time. "Oh—there she is again. She probably forgot something. I'll be right back."

I headed back into the front, and I swear I know how to walk, but I tripped over my foot and collided face-first with the door. I rubbed my nose, steadying my footing again, before I opened the door and my heart dropped into the pit of my stomach at the sight of Lyra Simmons there, holding a small, wrapped gift package, a bow on top.

"Oh—" I started, my throat tight. "Oh—oh! Oh my god. Hold on. Hold on. I wasn't expecting you."

"Piper—did you run into the door again?"

"No—yes—no—hold on." I shut the door.

Oh my god. Lyra was here.

I took a long breath, and I opened the door. It was still her. She was still here. My chest ached like I'd swallowed a knife. She was *here*. I'd forgotten how beautiful she was. It hadn't been forty-eight hours, but she was so pretty.

"*Lyra?*" My voice went too high. She smiled, eyes crinkling. She looked so cute in that scarf, earmuffs on. She held the package out again.

"Merry Christmas. Is your nose okay? It looks red."

"I—um—I hit it into the door just now." I took the package, my hands shaking. "Lyra? What are you doing here?"

"I..." She looked down. "I wanted to see you. For Christmas."

"But—I—you—"

"Sorry I took so long. I went to your house first. And I gave it time to allow that maybe you just couldn't hear me knocking..."

"You can't do this," I said, suddenly halfway between pouting and furious. "You can't do this! You just broke my heart *two days ago* and now you're here to remind me how pretty you are and how much I like you—"

"I like you, too," she said, taking my hand in hers, and my heart jumped so high it entered orbit. "I like you quite a lot, as a matter of fact. And the more I think about it, the more I feel like I belong here—that this is where I've really first felt like I belong."

I stared at her for a long, long time, my breath shaky, my heart pounding, before I breathed, "Lyra... I am the absolute worst at reading between the lines, so I need you to be very, very explicit. Are you saying you want to stay here? With—with me?"

She smiled wider. "If you're looking for Christmas Committee in the off-season."

"But—your job—"

"I have savings. And I'm in high demand now. I can negotiate remote work somewhere, even if it's not as high as my boss would pay me to come in."

I pursed my lips, every part of me stretched to breaking daring to hope. "I... um... I don't think we have the budget for a year-round Christmas Committee, you know."

"Ah, well." She relaxed. "Is the position of girlfriend open, then?"

"What—as if it wouldn't be? You think I'd have gotten another girlfriend that quickly? Who do you think I am, Cari Fletcher?"

"Someone's immersed in lesbian culture all of a sudden. It was a bit more rhetorical, Piper. What I'm saying is, I don't know if I'm staying forever or just for now, but... what I know is that I want to be with you. My life's more fun with you.

My life has a lot more meaning with you. And it makes me happy when I get to see you in the mornings. So... I don't have a forever plan. But in the now, I want to be here, and I want to be with you."

"Oh my god, you awful, terrible, no-good wretched and the worst ever human being," I said, falling on her and pulling her into a kiss that made me dizzy because it was *so* good and so right and I'd missed her *so* much even though it had only been a day and a half. She wrapped her arms around my waist and held me against her, and I kissed her like she was the only thing in the world and I was going to fall apart into pieces if I had to stop kissing her for one second, but I pulled away just long enough to look her in the eyes. "You can't play with a girl's heart like that, you know?"

"I know. I'm the worst. But to apologize, I'll stay with you as long as you'll have me. And if that's not enough, I got you a peppermint mocha, and the present."

"Oh! A peppermint mocha actually sounds wonderful. What present?"

"It's in your hand, sweetheart."

"Oh my god, it's in my hand. Oh, that's really embarrassing." I clasped it to my chest. "Can I open it now?"

"Is there any chance maybe I can come in first? It's a little cold."

"Oh my god, we're in the doorway. I forgot. I'm sorry. I'm a mess right now."

She laughed, pressing a kiss against my lips, and I was whole again, in all the little ways I always knew I was supposed to be. "I like you the way you are," she said, softly. "Sugarsquish."

"Oh, please. You can't embarrass me with that one anymore. I've become impervious."

"Mm. You've come a long way."

"I know," I laughed, tears sparkling in my eyes before I kissed her again, because no amount of kissing her would ever, ever, ever be enough.

Luckily I could take all the time I wanted to try kissing her enough, now.

Epilogue
LYRA

"Lyra," Piper's sing-song voice said, and I felt the mattress shift underneath me. "Darling, wake up. It's snowing!"

"It's winter. It does that." I reached for the blankets, but she caught my hand, rolling on top of me.

"Wake up! C'mon, we can watch the snow together!"

I woke up. Not because it was snowing, but because Piper was on top of me, and at this angle I could clearly see she wasn't wearing a bra. "Good morning," I said, and she snorted, a smile on her lips.

"C'mon. I'm up here."

"I can tell. All of you looks very good up there on top of me."

She kissed my forehead. "If you like my boobs that much, I can always show you if you get up."

"I think we have work to do, and if you go flashing me at this time of the morning, we both know where it's heading."

She laughed, lifting up her shirt. Sure enough, she was... definitely not wearing a bra. It wasn't like I was a simple woman, but I stared. "Work can wait."

"Didn't you want to watch the snow?"

"It'll still be snowing..." She bit her lip, a flush spreading over her cheeks, and that look in her eyes did it for me.

It was a *fantastic* way to wake up. With all the festival preparation going on lately, we hadn't gotten to have sex for over a week now, and Piper always released like a coil wound tight after too long without it. And I loved how loud she got when she released like that.

After quick warm showers, we arrived still breathless and satisfied for breakfast at the kitchen table—this place I'd called home for the past year now, ever since Piper and I agreed I could just stay here with her *while I looked for a better place to stay than that rental,* and then just... never really did. Moving in together by default somehow felt a lot easier, and living with Piper this past year had felt as natural as anything.

Leave it to Piper to make everything feel natural, spontaneous, and a lot of fun on top of it.

And of course, Piper moaned with satisfied delight when she bit into a croissant, leaning from her chair and nestling against my side watching the snow fall in the soft glow of the Christmas lights, still most of the light with dawn only a faint glow on the horizon.

"We didn't get any snow for the festival last year," she said. "It's going to be extra magical."

"Here I was thinking the fact that the buildings aren't falling apart this time was the special part."

"That's a good bonus." She kissed my cheek. "Do you need to go through your godawful emails again? We've got loads to do before the festival starts."

"I told them I'd be out of office for the rest of the month."

She shoved my shoulder. "Oh my god. Look at you, taking off from work!"

"Hey, I'm too valuable to fire now," I laughed. "Ever since they started calling me *community rebuilder Lyra Simmons,* I knew I was unfireable. I guess taking a week and a half off for Christmas isn't exactly scandalous behavior, but I'm still grateful for it."

"You *are* community rebuilder Lyra Simmons, darling. You've got companies trying to poach you every week. Women coming in and falling at your feet pleading for you to take them."

"I think you may be exaggerating."

"Either way, I'm glad you took off just for little old me and our celebrations." Her smile strained. "Now I also have bad news, um... apparently my parents volunteered to help with the setup today."

"Ah. Well. I don't know how we got by without their hands-on help last year."

She hung her head. "Do you think we can bring, like... a Lego set to distract them with?"

"No need," I laughed. "We'll just ask them to figure out the best color ribbons to put on each stall, and they'll spend the whole morning debating between green and gold."

"You say that, but I know they'll find a problem *somehow*."

When we got to the town center, Piper's parents were among the staff to meet us there, Louisa bundled up in two separate scarves, earmuffs, a coat and mittens, and Charles wearing an Ebenezer Scrooge-chic outfit that only made him look more like he was three times his wife's age. Still, even here waiting in the cold for the other volunteers to arrive, they were gazing at each other like they were the whole world, laughing together, and for a minute, I felt warm and fuzzy inside. Over the past year, I'd seen how much Piper took after them—she'd clearly internalized their model for a relationship, and even a year into living together, she still gazed at me like I'd hung the moon. Tender caresses, always laughing together, a million little pet names and all the adoring *yes, darlings*—all these mushy little things I'd never realized I could be so obsessed with.

She'd been so nervous the first time she'd told me she loved me—she'd asked me to come into the living room with her with a gravity in her expression and struggled for half an hour to actually say it, talking around it in increasing nervous high pitches and talking too quickly. I'd probably have been scared to death of what horrible news she might have been trying to work up to telling me, if I hadn't already heard her rehearsing saying it in the bathroom earlier that week. When she blurted that she loved me and collapsed face-first into the sofa to bury her face, I'd just patted her shoulder gently and told her I loved her too. She was adorable like that, and it was adorable watching the way she melted into a puddle on the couch burying herself in three different blankets and pillow when I told her the reason I wasn't surprised was because I'd heard her practicing it.

"You could have said it first, then!" she said, muffled under her blankets.

"I think it was important for you to say it."

She was quiet for a long time before, finally, she popped her head out from under the blanket, all just to throw a pillow at me and retreat back under her blankets. "I mean... maybe."

I'd kissed the top of her head through the blanket. "I love you."

"Okay. Fine. Fine, you'll always be able to get out of anything at all by saying that. You could lose my car and tell me you love me and I'd forget all about the car. I guess I'm not that different from my mom after all."

"How do you lose a car?"

"I don't know. Ask my dad."

I'd thought it was a hypothetical situation. Somehow, I suspected neither of her parents even really remembered it.

Admittedly, I had used the *I love you though* card to get out of a few things over the past year. But she'd had just as much power. I think we were about even, and I wasn't mad about it. Life was more fun with someone who didn't keep score or hold grudges and just loved, loved, loved. I still didn't understand how they were still alive, but I kind of got the dynamic of Piper's parents by now.

It took clearing my throat three times, standing there in the snow four feet away from them, before they noticed me. "Oh!" Louisa said, lighting up. "Oh, look, dear, it's Lyra. What are the odds of running into you here?"

I smiled. "Nearly a hundred percent, Louisa. Piper and I are the organizers for this."

She cocked her head. "The organizers for what?"

Charles nudged her side. "The festival, dear."

"Oh! Oh, I'm so silly. The festival. Right."

"Yes," Charles said, beaming. "Only two days away now."

I cleared my throat. "It's, er... it's actually today, Charles."

"Oh!" Louisa put a hand to her mouth. "Oh, that means we didn't plan Olive's party in time. Oh well. After Christmas."

Poor girl. Then again, I wondered if she'd even noticed. "What's her party for?"

Louisa beamed. "She dropped out of school!"

"Oh... um. That's great! I guess. Congratulations?"

"She's pursuing bigger dreams." Louisa puffed out her chest. It, uh... well, I was happy to see she was happy for her daughter.

"What are those bigger dreams of hers?"

She cocked her head. "Oh, um… I didn't think to ask. Probably napping more. She's asleep right now."

Well, set your goals in line with your dreams and all that.

The setup went by quicker this year than last—we'd actually been prepared this year, and we'd put up decorations the day after Thanksgiving. The shops had evened out over the past year—most of the popups closed and moved away, but a few stayed, and the developing area drew in some new interest. The town center was up to half capacity in the off season now, and with the popups ready for the Christmas season again this year, we'd packed every shopfront, every inch of stall space, and every available square foot of the mall, which had come alive as a community gathering place again over the past year.

Plus, we had a couple more people to help out this time. Turned out people really did just need the promise of things changing—a few families moved back into Castle Hollow, taking advantage of the cheap housing, and after the tourism board's glowing recommendation of Castle Hollow as a cozy small town that had Christmas charm in spades, we'd gotten a steady stream of newcomers from all walks of life.

We were a little overloaded with volunteers, but it was hardly the worst problem to have. Especially when we needed a few full-time to make sure Piper's parents didn't wander off with anything important.

But when we finished the setup and the church bells chimed noon, music filled the air, and Piper and I stepped back to take it all in—the sights, the sounds, the smells of Christmas, once again.

"I'm exhausted," Piper sighed, falling against my side, where we stood at the front of the town hall looking out over the festival arrangements around the Christmas tree in the square. "Pick me up and carry me home, darling. I need to sleep."

"We'd get about fifteen feet before you decided something you wanted to go do instead, my love."

"I know." She nuzzled her face against my shoulder. "Hey, um... thanks."

"No problem. Dare I ask what for?"

"Sticking around. Believing in me. All this was only possible because you believed in me when nobody else did. And I'm really happy you're here and that I get to love you, because you're amazing."

I rested my head against hers, still just a little blown away how much she made my heart flutter with things like this all the time. Her earrings—the ones with the subtle snowflake design that I'd gotten her last Christmas—pressed against my shoulder, and I felt mine, the golden-ratio ones she'd gotten me last year, pressing against her head. Who knew I'd end up such a pile of mush for a girl?

"Thanks for having me," I said. "You did your work as head of the cultural committee extremely well."

She covered up a giggle. "Thanks. I take my work seriously, you know."

Gloria's voice from behind made me jump. "I love seeing you two be cute," she said, and Piper pulled away and whirled back on her.

"You and Whitney both are too old to be sneaking around like a ninja dishing out heart attacks," she said. "Where did you even come from?"

"Whitney's been teaching me a few things. Just wanted to congratulate you on another happy festival. And another happy year together with the happy love of your life. To think, you tried telling me you were straight." She laughed. "Really, who's buying that?"

Piper hung her head. "I was, for a while..."

"Thanks for stopping by, Gloria," I said. "I know you're busy lately."

"I am, but of course I have time to step away and look after my most precious little coworker." She cleared her throat. "By that I mean I blew off the work, but I'll deal with it later."

Piper stiffened. "Gloria! You can't just... oh, forget it. We'll get it done later."

"Little taskmaster," Gloria laughed, turning back to her. "Say. Bolton told me he's not going to run for mayor again."

Piper went wide-eyed. "Really?"

"Yeah. He says he might as well give it up, since the town is actually going places now and he just wanted to be mayor while there was nothing to do aside from routine paperwork and feeling important about it."

I scratched the back of my head. "He's always been very... honest."

"I told him you'd make a good mayor," Gloria said, and Piper stared for a solid five seconds before she burst out laughing.

"Uh—no. No way. Not a chance. Me? I'm not the type."

"Really—" Gloria started, but Piper shook her head.

"No, really. I'm happy being cultural committee."

"After everything that happened last year, I'm sure you'd be uncontested."

She rubbed the back of her neck, looking down with a faint flush across her cheeks. "Um... I think you give me a little too much credit. But it wouldn't matter if I'd win a hundred percent of the vote. I prefer a position that lets me be a little more... spontaneous. That lets me be creative with my tasks and get Lyra involved too, whenever she wants to be a part. Work that lets me stay home and just spend the day with Lyra or go visit my family together whenever I need to recharge and reconnect. You know?" She looked back out to the square, the festival still filling up with more people arriving—so many more families than last year, people with their kids running around laughing. "What I've dreamed of is just... making this place feel special for people. And this is the place where I can do that the best. I look forward to seeing who's going to be the new mayor. I hope we can work well together."

I slipped an arm around her waist, trying not to look *too* smug with how proud I was of my girlfriend. I wasn't sure I managed.

Gloria stared for a second before she leaned back against the wall of the town hall, a smile on her face. "Look at you, taking everything I said to heart."

"No, um..." Piper cleared her throat. "No, I said I'm not doing it."

"Not that, you silly goose. Turning down the promotion, the big grownup responsibilities that look good on paper, for the things that light you up. You really are a smart girl."

Piper relaxed. "Oh... yeah. I remember when you told me that." She cast a sidelong glance at me, and then away, flushing. "Yeah, I definitely remember that."

I was missing something. I was also pretty sure I wasn't supposed to ask right now what I was missing.

"Well, I'm happy for you," Gloria said. "The town will do well with you on the cultural committee. And besides, the mayorship is probably staying close."

Piper cocked her head. "How do you mean?"

"Your sister's running."

Piper dropped her phone. "She's—*what?* Oh my god, no. Oh my god, she can't do that. Isn't she too young?"

I suppressed a laugh, struggling to keep a straight face. So, those were her bigger dreams. I wondered how often the mayor could take naps.

Gloria beamed. "Not anymore! She told Bolton about it and he said it'd be hilarious, so he lowered the age limit to run."

"Oh my god. He can't just run things based on what sounds funny!" Piper raked her fingers through her hair. "Oh, she *cannot* be mayor. Who else is running?"

"Don't know if anybody wants to run against her. Whole town hall's excited about having the Fairway sisters both in charge of things."

"Oh, no, no, no. This can't be happening."

"I think it'll be fun seeing what kind of ideas she has for the town..."

"She has no idea how to run a town! She has no idea how to run anything!"

I cleared my throat. "I know a few things about the law and properties. I can, er... step in where she needs me."

Piper buried her face in her hands. "I cannot believe this."

"Oh, what do you know," came Olive's voice, right on cue, as she slouched up the steps from the coffee shop nearby, a massive iced coffee in hand. "Piper's all high-strung about something."

"There's our bright-eyed candidate!" Gloria clasped her hands together. "How are you doing?"

"Olive, you can't be serious," Piper said, whirling on her. "Why are you *running* for *mayor?*"

Olive shrugged. "I thought it sounded cool. And I figure if I'm the mayor, then no one can tell me what to do."

"That's literally how nothing works," Piper said.

I put a hand on her shoulder. "Don't worry," I said. "I'm sure Olive won't, er... do anything too drastic while she's in power."

Because she probably wasn't going to do a thing. But I wasn't saying that out loud.

"I can't believe this," Piper groaned, and Olive just walked past her.

"She complains so much... I'm going to get a snack."

Even after a full evening of walking through the festival hand-in-hand, laughing together with old friends, and picking up way too many shopping bags of a million different gifts for family and friends, Piper still crashed face-first into the couch when we got back to her house.

"I cannot believe *Olivia Fairway* might end up Mayor of Castle Hollow," she groaned. I went past her to the kitchen, starting the tea kettle without even having to ask anymore.

"Quite an accomplished political family, you Fairways," I said, calling from the kitchen.

"She's not going to accomplish anything. Except maybe forcing through a new regulation to introduce mandatory nap times."

"People generally work too hard anyway. Nap times don't sound half bad."

"God, you're campaigning on her platform." But she was smiling wryly once I brought peppermint tea for the two of us out to the living room and we sat close together on the couch, Piper nestling up against my side. "I guess at least I can rest assured she'll just hand over any important tasks to you and me instead of making a decision based on what's funniest. Might be an improvement over Bolton."

"Look at you, finding the bright side."

"I'm ever the optimist, darling." She laughed, nuzzling against my side. "So, how's the festival hold up to last time so far for you?"

"Better."

"Yeah?"

I nodded, cradling my tea close.

After all, as much as last year was a thrill and a triumph, and as much as it felt new and magical and a Christmas miracle through and through, this time was special. Not because there were more people, not because everything was in better condition, not because of all the families and the laughter of children in the air, not because we knew this time the town was safe, once and for all.

This year was a lot better, because this time, I was experiencing it as my home. And this time, I was experiencing it alongside the woman I wanted to spend forever with. I'd been so careful hedging my bets last year, saying things like *I don't know if I'll stay, but I want to be with you for the now,* but once I'd gone in headfirst, I knew as well as anything that nothing had ever felt like home quite like Castle Hollow by Piper's side.

I loved this woman—really, really did love her. And I couldn't wait to see how much more fun the festival would be next year, too.

"Much better," I said, sinking back in the sofa and watching the snowflakes fall, drifting, dancing down to join the soft white that covered the ground.

"What is?"

"You forgot the conversation topic, didn't you?"

"I was thinking about something else."

"Don't worry about it, darling."

She laughed, sinking into my side. "If you say so."

The End

Celebrate the holidays together with your favorite authors, with the **Tis the Season Holiday Collection**: nine sweet and tropey Christmas romance novellas to bring light and life this holiday season.

Check out the full collection at **lilyseabrooke.com/tis-the-season**, cozy up by the fire, and enjoy a sweet Christmas celebration, from all of us.

Happy holidays!